FATED

A Second Chance Romance

HEARTS

It's like Fifty Shades meets Gabriel's Inferno meets The Boy Who Sneaks In My Bedroom Window and I freaking loved it!
-Lexa, Goodreads

USA TODAY
BESTSELLING AUTHOR
Sophie Monroe

xoxo
Sophie Monroe

The author acknowledges the use of the following: The Body Shop, Dolce & Gabbana, Valentino, Prada, Jacuzzi, Four Seasons, Park 75 restaurant, Tiffany & Co., iPhone, GQ, Duval, Target, Jeep, Duane Reid, Starbucks, Google, Kitchen-Aid, Corona, My Darkest Days, Infiniti, Bluetooth, Victoria's Secret, Splenda, Jack Daniels, Magnum, Buckcherry

Contact:

sophiemonroe007@hotmail.com
www.sophiemonroewrites.com

www.facebook.com/sophiemonroewrites

Writing a book is an adventure. To begin with, it is a toy and an amusement; then it becomes a mistress, and then it becomes a master, and then a tyrant. The last phase is that just as you are about to be reconciled to your servitude, you kill the monster, and fling it out to the public.

"The whole point of being alive is to evolve into the complete person you were intended to be." ~Oprah Winfrey

I woke to a warm, overly dominating body pressed up against me. It belonged to my best friend and boyfriend, Noah. We had met ten years ago when he was eight and I was six. We'd been best friends ever since. We only started dating a little over a year ago, but I honestly don't know what I would do without him. He's my sanity in an insane world… my rock.

We've been secretly sleeping like this every night for the past five years… ever since the night of my eleventh birthday. When I know my mom is down for the count, I sneak over here to sleep. I've always been able to evade her and sneak back home before she

7

wakes up. To say that my mom and I don't get along would be an understatement. We're like oil and water, cats and dogs, fire and ice.

Over the last couple of years, I've outgrown being shy and awkward. I grew into my body, curves and all. I finally stopped growing at a little over five foot seven. My blonde hair is down to the middle of my back and has natural highlights from the Georgia sun. Genetics blessed me with my dad's oval green eyes and porcelain skin. Thankfully, I didn't look like my mother, except for the blonde hair.

Noah's *hot!* He's a little over six feet tall and muscular, but not too buff. He has the most beautiful chiseled features, a square jaw, and strong nose. His piercing, blue eyes compliment his short, dark hair. His lips are my favorite, though; they're just so kissable!

"Morning, Jules," he whispered in his raspy morning voice. I love that voice more than anything. I looked at his messy case of bedhead and his breathtaking smile and wished that we could stay in this moment forever. I smiled back as he moved me onto his chest so that we were face to face. I nuzzled in the crook of his neck, breathing in his cologne, and snuggled closer. Thankfully, since my mom had stayed out last night, I didn't have to worry about sneaking back. Mornings like this were my favorite.

8

I closed my eyes until the alarm went off and reluctantly dragged myself from his bed. He kissed my head and helped me out the window and I headed across the lawn, back to my house to get ready for school. As soon as I opened my window, a set of blood red claws dug into my arm, yanking me inside.

"Where the fuck have you been?" my mom, Abigail, yelled. She'd been waiting for me, and it wasn't because she was concerned for my safety. "You little whore, I asked you a question!"

"Since when do you care?" I spat.

She slapped my face, making my skin sting. I was used to this kind of treatment by now. I'd been taking care of myself since I was eight when my dad took a job in England.

"You were with the Sinclair boy, weren't you? How many years have you been fucking him now?"

I didn't reply. I found it best to bite my tongue where she was concerned.

My mother's polished appearance was only a facade. She was a vicious woman who resented me. *As if I would have chosen to be born into this family.* She grabbed a picture frame off my end table, the one Noah had given me for my eleventh birthday, and tossed it to the ground. The glass shattered. She huffed away,

9

slamming the door behind her, leaving me to do what I do best - pick up the broken pieces.

I quickly picked up the pieces that I could and placed them on my dresser. I would try to glue some of it back together later. I pulled myself together and headed to my bathroom to shower. I took extra care applying foundation to ensure the slap mark was covered. I dressed in a black leather pleated skirt that showed off my long legs, a ribbed gray tank top, knee high Doc Martens, and a cardigan.

I hoped my outfit would distract Noah from my face. Despite my best efforts, though, he noticed.

"She hit you again, didn't she?" He ran his lightly ran his fingertips over my cheek. I nodded. "Jules, we can just run away. I'm eighteen now. We can start over, just the two of us."

"You know we can't. You're graduating in less than seven months. Plus, you know wherever we go, she'll hunt me down like a bloodhound. It will just make everything worse," I said sadly.

"She only cares because she doesn't want your dad to cut her off financially. Just think about it, *please*. I'll make it happen if it's what you want."

I told him that I would think about it, but we both knew damn well I couldn't actually go through with it. Things at home had been getting worse since my parents finally decided to divorce two years ago and my dad couldn't reel her in any longer. His visits had always been sporadic, but after the divorce, they stopped altogether. It left me to fend for myself.

Abigail Kline was selfish, self-centered, and egotistical. If it didn't work for her, she wasn't happy. She was rarely ever happy. I often wondered if she always acted like this, or if it was just after I'd come into the picture. I was an accident, and she never let me forget it. She had recently started dating a much older man named Clark Donahue. He was from New York and traveled here a lot on business. I liked when he'd fly her there to visit because it made my life easier. It wasn't often enough, though.

I was thankful that we had a couple classes together. Just spending time with him made my day better. We both took mostly AP classes and were working extremely hard to keep our grades up so we could get into good colleges. He wanted to be a lawyer, and I wanted to be a journalist. Since I could work from pretty much anywhere, I was willing to go wherever he was. We had plans for the future.

At the beginning of our relationship, we had decided that we were going to wait to have sex until we were married. If we had our choice, it would be as soon as I was eighteen. But, something happened that day that changed everything…

11

We walked in my front door after ensuring that my mom's car wasn't there. I was laughing as Noah was attempting to tickle me. He left our book bags by the front door, and we headed to the kitchen. I would always make us a snack before we started doing our homework. There was a note from my mother on the kitchen counter. I assumed it was just her telling me that she would be gone again. It wasn't.

Julia,

Your recent behavior is completely unacceptable and out of control. With this, Clark and I have decided that we would be much better moving to New York. You will find a plane ticket dated one-week from today. The movers will be here starting tomorrow to move our things into storage.

Do NOT even think about trying to run away either. I will track you down and you will be VERY sorry!

I sunk to the floor and put my head between my knees. Noah took the letter out of my hands and read it quickly. The saddest part was she would hunt me down and make my life hell, even though I was a burden to her.

"We can still run away if you want to." His blue eyes stared mine. I wanted nothing more, but I knew there was no escaping her wrath.

Two more years… I kept repeating it in my head. After that, I wouldn't have to see her ever again if I didn't want to. "We can't. She'll find me and then we'll both be in trouble. She's not going to let this go." Tears slid down my face as the realization hit.

He sat next to me on the floor and pulled me close. Resting my head on his lap, the thought of leaving him behind was making me physically sick. I couldn't imagine a life without Noah. He was my everything and not in the childish, puppy love way. What we shared was so real. The kind of love you felt in your soul. My mind raced as my anxiety skyrocketed. Noah's hand slid up and down my spine. It wasn't enough to calm me completely, but my tears started to slow.

"I love you, Jules."

Sitting up, I straddled his waist and began kissing him. The kiss deepened as my body started to respond. I wanted him. After all the time we waited, it seemed like it was time. It also seemed like it was now or never...

"I love you too, so much," I said as I pulled back. "I'm ready."

"I don't know, Jules," he sighed apprehensively. "It seems spur of the moment."

13

"I do know I don't want to wait anymore. Honestly, I'm surprised we've made it this long. I want you to be my first, my only."

"You're sure," he asked. Looking at my face for any doubt, I nodded.

Wanting to make it memorable, in typical Noah fashion, I quickly changed course. Knowing that my departure was he booked a room at the Four Seasons in Atlanta. We would spend our last night together there before he took me to the airport. We would be separated for longer than a week, for the first time ever.

That week, we spent as much time together as possible. I stayed with him every night, as usual. Five days later, we went to the hotel. As he went to put our bags into the bedroom, I used the bathroom to get ready for dinner. He'd made us reservations for the Park 75 restaurant at eight. I put on all black lace lingerie that I'd picked out at a local boutique and dressed in a sleeveless leather and lace sheath dress that Noah had picked out for me. I paired it with black wedges and pulled my hair in a half-bouffant, curling some of the pieces for a rocker chick look. I applied some light makeup and finished the look with red lipstick. I felt beautiful.

Picking up my clutch bag, I took a deep breath and headed for the door. Glancing at Noah, who was dressed in a charcoal gray

14

suit with a white shirt and black tie. *He looked breathtaking* as he stood there, grinning at me. He told me I looked gorgeous, but he would have said that if I was dressed in a potato sack.

He leaned down and kissed my cheek, before taking my hand and walking down to the restaurant. I ordered lemon thyme chicken with grilled asparagus and mashed potatoes, and Noah ordered the beef tenderloin with béarnaise sauce and hand cut fries. We ate mostly in silence. Neither of us addressed the fact that I was leaving. We knew it was going to happen, but we didn't want it to spoil our special night. After dinner, we shared a peanut butter lava cake. When we were done eating, he pulled his chair closer to mine and produced a ring from inside his suit pocket. It was a sterling silver ring inscribed with *Faith. Love. My Jujube,* his nickname for me.

"This is my promise to you. I will be with you, wherever you are. If you need me, I'll come for you. No matter what… I love you, Jules." He kissed my cheek. Tears blurred my vision. His thoughtfulness was usually overwhelming to me. Even after all these years, he never ceased to amaze me. The waiter came with the check and Noah settled our bill. It was finally time.

We went back to our room and made love for the first time. It was perfect, and nothing like I'd expected it to be. It was as if we had done it a hundred times. Like we were made for each other. As if we needed more assurance.

15

Waking up the next day was hard, reality was setting in. I was leaving. I tried my hardest to stay in this moment with Noah for as long as I could. Packing up my suitcase, I left my iPod and a book handy for the plane ride. I tossed my hair up in a ponytail and put on a pair of skinny jeans and a t-shirt that were both fashionable and functional. A million butterflies formed in my stomach as the minutes ticked by. The thought of running away kept popping up. I squashed it down, but I didn't want to leave him, either.

After check out, we headed straight to the airport. We promised to see each other as much as possible. He promised to come to New York after graduation and get a job so we could be close again. I hoped I'd be able to leave and move in with him. I'd happily live in a closet with him rather than a mansion with Abigail.

"Promise we'll stick together," I said to him.

"Like pages in a porn magazine," he promised, making me laugh.

We kissed for the last time…

That was ten years ago.

Chapter One: Porn Star Dancing

Present Day

"Noah," Professor Mitchell called during attendance.

I felt the sudden urge to look around the room, just to see if he was here. To this day, every time I heard that name, I wanted to run away. Although I knew it wasn't 'my Noah,' it still burned. Over the years, the pain had numbed but never truly subsided. Even though it had been almost ten years since I'd last seen him, I still couldn't forget him.

Snapping out of it, I quickly turned my attention back to the podium. I couldn't wait to finish my last semester of graduate school. A day I'd been impatiently waiting for the past two years.

I trudged through the rest of the day, making sure I stopped for a latte before heading to work. I worked at Double D's, an upscale gentleman's club located in the center of Manhattan. Most of the men who frequent the club have more money than sense. They come for business dinners, bachelor parties, or any reason they can come up with. I enjoy it, though. Since my dad cut me off at eighteen, I needed a way to support myself. Working here, I made enough money to get by comfortably. Plus, it didn't interfere with school. *Win, win.*

I was dressed and waiting off to the side of the stage.

"You know you love 'em; you know you want to bang 'em. I know I do. Introducing... our devilishly own Felony and Miss Demeanor," Keith, the club's skeevy MC, crooned into the microphone.

Stepping on shiny, black stiletto onto the raised platform, I peeked out at the crowd. It was a full house tonight, which meant fantastic tips. I sauntered onto the stage with my best friend and roommate, Ellie. Except, when we were here, we weren't Jules and Ellie; I was Felony, and she was Miss Demeanor.

When we'd moved to New York, my mom was in a hurry to get rid of me, so she sent me to boarding school. That's where I met Ellie. She was a fiercely protective, petite little spitfire. We connected right away and have been attached at the hip ever since.

Our song, 'Porn Star Dancing' by My Darkest Days, was pumping through the speakers and making the floor beneath shake. I loved the thrill of being up here; it filled me with adrenaline and made me feel liberated. I surveyed the dimly lit room, which was mostly lit up from the stage. The front of the stage was lined with stools. The rest of the club had tables and a couple booths. It also housed an expansive bar. I made eye contact with a few of the patrons before turning my attention to the shiny, silver pole.

I tossed my hair around and started swinging. I teasingly untied my black patent leather bikini top, giving the crowd a peek before tossing it offstage. A regular of mine, Russell, slipped a couple hundred-dollar bills into my boy-shorts. He was handsome for an older man. He had sparkly, blue eyes and a shaved head like Mr. Clean. He was sweet as pie and offered me a multitude of extravagant gifts to be his girlfriend. (He was only partly kidding.) I kissed the top of his head, leaving a red lipstick print, and gave him a wink before turning my attention back to the rest of the crowd. Ellie was working the other side of the stage like the porn star princess she was. She had already lost her top and had a group from a bachelor party tossing money at her.

They started a drunken chant. "Take it off!" She stood, shaking her finger at them.

19

Biting my lip, I made my way to the top of the pole before lowering my body upside down in an exotic spin. The electricity of the room was on high tonight and before long the song switched to AC/DC's 'Shook Me All Night Long.' Ellie and I did our rehearsed dance before exiting the stage. The room erupted into cheers for an encore. Once we were in the break room, I unbuckled my black patent leather seven-inch spike heels and tossed them into my bag. After working here for the past few years, I could probably run a marathon in them.

Changing into street clothes, I grabbed a makeup remover wipe from the vanity to take off the excess eye shadow. I was relieved we were done for the night because I was exhausted.

"How'd you make out?" I asked Ellie.

"I made four hundred and forty-four dollars. Not bad for our eight-minute segment." She gave me a high five. "How about you?"

I pulled out my money and counted it. Russell gave me four hundred and with the other money, I got I'd made a total of $721.

"Seven hundred and twenty-one smackers." I winked, stuffing it into my bra.

"Holy shit! Not bad, chicky. We should do a shot to celebrate. Brad's working the bar tonight." She grinned.

20

I didn't like to mix business with pleasure, but Ellie had a massive crush on Brad, so I knew I wasn't getting out of it. "All right, but just one. I have class early tomorrow."

"Yay." She hooked her arm in mine, as we headed to get a seat at the bar.

"Hello, sexy ladies," Brad said, appraising us. "What can I get you?"

Brad was cute in a boy-next-door kind of way. He had dark blonde hair and brown eyes that crinkled when he smiled. He'd only been working here for about three months and seemed likable enough. I didn't really take the chance to get to know most of the people here, unlike Ellie.

"I'll have a slippery nipple," Ellie ordered, batting her fake eyelashes.

"I'll have a Corona with lemon, not lime," I ordered.

"You got it, sweet cheeks. That was one hell of a crowd out there." He looked at the bachelor party crowd as they were cheering obnoxiously at the current dancers.

"Eh. It was all right. We've had better," Ellie said.

21

He winked. "Are you ready for the huge one on Saturday? I can't believe they rented out the club for the night! Must have cost them a fortune."

"I'm sure it will be memorable, just like all the others," I said dryly. I loved the money from the bachelor parties, but they were all the same. They mostly consisted of a bunch of drunken men trying to get a piece of ass.

I finished my beer and left Ellie talking, or more like flirting, with Brad. I kissed her cheek and told her I would see her at home. I waved to Dan, who was the security guard that stood watch at the back door to the parking garage.

"Have a good evening, Miss Kline."

"You too, Dan, and will you call me Jules already?" I laughed.

I climbed into my Infiniti IPL G convertible, tossing my bag onto the passenger seat. I spent the thirty-minute drive home thinking about all the schoolwork that I had waiting for me. My mind started drifting to ten years ago, again. I pushed it out of my head.

I haven't spoken with my mother since a couple months after we moved to New York. During spring break, things got downright ugly with her, so bad that cops were involved. I left and never went back. I've been on my own ever since. I didn't like to think of that night, just like I didn't like to think of *Noah*. The one person whom I trusted more than anyone in the world, the one who ended up ripping my heart clean out of my chest and pulverized it in a blender.

Chapter Two:
Saturday Nights Alright

••◦•➤•◦•➤•◦•➤•◦•➤•◦•➤•◦•➤•◦•➤•◦•➤•◦•➤•◦•➤•◦•➤•◦••

The rest of the week passed quickly. My days revolved around school, and my nights revolved around work. I was busy trying to finish my thesis on *Romeo and Juliet* that was due at the end of the semester. I was getting my MA from Columbia University in English and Comparative Literature.

I spent most of the day typing away, so by the time I looked at the clock I realized it was already seven. I needed to get ready because we had that huge bachelor party tonight. The guy throwing it rented out the entire place. It was most likely some yuppie from the East Side with too much money on his hands. Hopefully, that would make it a good night for me. Ellie had already left to help Brad stock the bar. Though, chances were pretty good that they were busy getting it on in the supply closet.

Tossing my black-framed glasses onto my desk, I rubbed my tired eyes. After jumping into the shower, I hurried through it and toweled off quickly. Rummaging through my closet, I picked out a red lace panty and bustier set and a black, pleated leather skirt. I added a white button up shirt and threw on a pair of flats on the off chance I got pulled over on the way to work. That would make for an interesting story, not.

Tossing my signature black stilettos into my duffle bag, I headed from our tiny house in Amityville to the Big Apple. Thankfully, traffic was light, and I pulled into the parking garage of the club at quarter to eight. I greeted Dan as I walked through the back door into the break room.

Sitting at the vanity, I frantically applied my make-up. I teased my blonde hair, with black highlights, and added some silver glitter eye shadow. I opted for a nude lip-gloss over my regular red. I didn't like doing too much to my eyes and adding bright lips. To me, it just looked trashy, so I did one or the other. I changed my shoes and checked my panties.

Right before we were supposed to go on, Ellie came barreling in with a huge grin on her face. She looked incredible tonight. Her year-round tan, courtesy of a tanning booth, contrasted with the white in her outfit. She'd curled her black hair into thick curls that went down to the middle of her back and bounced with each step. She was in a white lace set with knee-high white leather boots. She always liked to dress like a bride for these things. I usually opted for the devil.

26

"Holy hotness! The crowd looks like a fucking *GQ* photo shoot! I mean, they are seriously yummy, Jules!" I rolled my eyes and laughed at her. I loved her dearly, but it didn't take much to impress her. I think even Steve Urkel could impress her if he tried hard enough.

She handed me a Ring-Pop. I gave her my *'what the hell'* look. Typical Ellie just laughed.

"I changed our opening song. You'll need it."

Our boss, Adam, came in to talk to us before we took the stage. He was dressed in his usual jeans and Double D's polo shirt. He was in his mid-thirties with brown hair and olive skin. I guess, by most people's standards, he would be considered a good-looking guy.

"Ladies. Looking delectable, as always." He smiled, looking us over. He often referred to us as "Adam's Angels."

"Thanks, Adam," Ellie purred. She'd had a thing for Adam when we started working here. Even more surprising was when he told her that he didn't sleep with any of the dancers. It was one of the things I admired about him. Unfortunately, that didn't stop him from perving.

"As you know, this group is paying a lot, and I mean *a lot,* of money for the full club experience. I expect you to give it to them. I've arranged for Preacher to be in the room with you, if they want a private dance, for your safety. Any problems, let me know."

"Will do," I said with a salute. I was an old pro at these events by now.

"All right, go make me some money." He slapped my ass, and I fought the urge to slap him in the face. I did feel a little guilty because he was an overall good guy. He almost couldn't help that he was a total perv.

Keith called our introduction, and we headed onto the stage. Instead of 'Porn Star Dancing,' Ellie had changed it to Nickelback's 'Something In Your Mouth.' I finally understood the need for the Ring-Pop. I took one side of the stage while Ellie took the other. They were a generous bunch for sure, and good-looking from what I could see. They were tossing twenties and fifties like our regulars threw fives and tens. I unzipped my skirt, letting it pool at my feet. It earned me a bunch of whistles and whoops and I gracefully kicked it off the stage. A Johnny Depp look-alike caught it. I winked at him. The guy next to him, a blonde, practically knocked him off his chair to grab it. The song changed to Theory of a Deadman's 'Bad Girlfriend.' I was having fun shaking my ass. I was doing it like my tuition was depending on it; it was.

Ellie and I met in the middle of the stage. She handed me a piece of paper. I unfolded it and read it quickly; it was clearly a guy's handwriting.

Gotta meet the hottie with the million-dollar body.

I rolled my eyes and walked over to her side of the stage. I started to dance when I froze in place. I had to grab the pole to keep from falling over. In front of me sat Noah Sinclair, the same boy who'd broken my heart ten years ago. He was looking better than ever. He looked just as shocked as I did. When my wits returned, I walked, okay I sprinted, off the stage. As soon as I was off stage, I started hyperventilating. If I wasn't worried about what was on the floor, I would have been on it.

Adam came storming out of his office, looking pissed. "What the hell are you doing? Get back out there, right now!"

"I can't," I barely managed to say. I could feel the beginning of tears burning my eyes.

"What the fuck do you mean you can't? You can, and you're going to, even if I have to drag you back out there myself. You're the best dancer I have. The guy throwing the party specifically booked the both of you." Ellie and I were the high rollers at the club. Most people asked for us by name, much like tonight.

29

"Adam, I can't. I know one of the guests. Please don't make me," I pleaded. "Have Willow go instead. Please... I'm begging you." The tears I had been holding in already started falling.

Adam didn't do tears. Frankly, I think they scared the shit out of him.

"Jailbait," He yelled, making me flinch. Willow came running out from the bar.

"Bossman," she replied.

Willow was a cute little thing with brown hair and big brown eyes. I always thought she looked a little like Ashley Greene. She got the nickname Jailbait because she was just eighteen. She danced from time to time when someone would call in sick.

"I need you to go out there and fill in for Jules."

"Are you all right? Did you hurt yourself?" she asked, noticing the tears.

"I'm fine," I lied.

She shimmied out of her shorts and tossed her tank in Adam's face, heading headed onto the stage. I swear he sniffed it. *Gross.* A couple minutes passed, and my breathing finally returned

30

to normal. I was rushing like hell to get out of there. I was taking my make-up off when I looked up and saw Noah in the mirror.

His blue eyes pierced into mine. "Jules?"

"No, I think you're mistaking me for someone else."

"Nice try, I'd know you anywhere, Jujube." *Dammit.*

"Do you need something? 'Cause I'm kinda busy right now," I snapped.

"Busy removing make-up?" He crossed his arms while leaning in the doorway.

"Very."

"Jules, please talk to me," he pleaded.

I refused to turn around and make eye contact again. "Oh, just like you talked to me after I left? You promised me, Noah! You were my lifeline!"

"What are you talking about?" He looked genuinely confused, but I wasn't backing down.

"After I left, you never called. You couldn't even send me a fucking text?" I felt my tears coming back, but my anger helped me suppress them.

"I texted you almost every day. And I did call, but every time I did, I got your voicemail. Which was always full, by the way. I assumed that *you* didn't want to talk to me anymore. I even flew up during spring break to win you back. Your mom said you were away, and that you'd moved on." He paused, as if he were remembering. "She said she would tell you I came. I was heartbroken."

I wondered if he was telling the truth, or if he just liked my 'million-dollar body.'

"I never got any messages from you. So don't you dare lie to me, Noah Sinclair! I carried my phone with me everywhere just in case. I needed you!"

I saw Dan pop his head in. When he saw that it was okay, he quickly closed the door.

"Why didn't you just call me?" he asked with a bitter edge in his voice.

"If you didn't want me anymore, I didn't want to seem desperate."

"I would never think you were desperate."

I turned my attention back to the mirror.

"Please talk to me." Seeing him grovel wasn't going to help my resolve. I was biting my lip and trying not to cry, again. I saw the blonde guy who'd tried to tackle the Johnny Depp look-alike. He came up behind Noah and put his arm around his shoulder.

"Come on, bro, the parties a'waitin.' I paid good money for you to have a memorable night." He slapped Noah on the back. My heart sank even more. *Noah was the bachelor.*

"Not now, Jackson. Can't you see I'm in the middle of something? Go back out there. I'll see you in a bit," Noah barked.

"Aren't you going to introduce us?" his friend asked, gesturing to me.

"No," Noah said flatly.

"Come on, man, don't be like that. Hoes before bros and all that."

Noah slapped him in the chest with the back of his hand. He looked at me. "Jules, this is Jackson Richardson. Jackson, this is Jules."

"Jules? Like *the* Jules?" He looked incredulously at Noah.

"The one and only," Noah said, embarrassed.

33

"Holy shit!" hes said about five octaves too high. "I mean, excuse me, it's nice to meet you, Jules." He came into the room and offered his hand; we shook. "Wow, I can't believe I finally get to meet you. I've heard *a lot* about you. Everything was always like 'Jules used to do that,' or 'Jules liked that,' and now you're here. Just wow!"

I noticed how he said, 'used to.' Jackson reminded me of an underwear model and was undoubtedly a charmer.

"Jackson, I love you, man, but please go. I need a few minutes with Jules," Noah begged.

"Oh, I get it. One last time for old time's sake. Your secret's safe with me." He winked and walked out of the room. Noah was blushing.

"You're an ass," Noah yelled after him.

He tried to take a step further into the dressing room, and I put my hand up. "Don't even think about it."

"I wouldn't do that to you, Jules."

"You're damn right you wouldn't because I wouldn't let you. I'm not yours, Noah, not anymore." He winced, like I'd slapped him. "Who's the lucky gal?" I sneered.

"Her name is Carrie Collins." His tone was glum. He didn't look like a happy bachelor. He was getting closer, and I could smell the familiar scent that was all Noah.

"Well, congratulations. I really need to get going; it was nice seeing you. Take care of yourself, Noah." I needed to get out of there. I felt like I was going to have a breakdown at any second. Grabbing my bag, I pushed past him to get to the exit.

"Jules!" he yelled. "Jujube!" I flinched when he called me Jujube. I didn't turn around because I knew that if I did I'd never want to walk away.

He looked the same, but better. He'd grown into a man, a very good-looking man. Luckily, Dan was standing by the door. There was no way Noah was pushing past him, not unless he wanted a concussion.

Starting my car, I sped into the crisp New York City night before I let the tears fall. I hadn't cried like that in years. By the time I arrived home, I was a freaking mess. I showered and slipped into my sick jammies, the ones with sheep on them. Climbing into bed, it wasn't even ten o'clock yet. I was hoping sleep would come quickly. It was a futile wish.

Chapter Three:
Your Love Is My Drug

I was reliving my nightmare from ten years ago when I felt someone climb into bed with me. Screaming at the top of my lungs, it brought me back to *that* night. The night that I started sleeping at Noah's.

I bolted upright. "It's just me; relax." Ellie whispered. "I heard what happened. I thought you would be happy to see him. Why didn't you come get me?"

I looked at my alarm. It was after two in the morning. I wasn't interested in rehashing the evening or delving into my past. "I just wanted to leave. I needed to get out of there. It was horrible. Ellie."

"So that's Noah, huh?" She raised her eyebrow.

"Yep," I said flatly, rubbing my eyes.

"He's good looking. I mean *really* good looking."

Even I could admit that he looked amazing. He looked like Noah 2.0. "Can we stop talking about this now? I'm exhausted," I whined.

Ellie got the look on her face that she would get anytime she had to tell me something bad. The same look she had when our hamster Rhino died. "You're going to kill me, Jules." She took a deep breath. "When my set was over, he asked me for a private dance. I hopped right off the stage and went to the room, so I didn't even know you'd left. He told me who he was, and I kinda sorta gave him your phone number. I didn't know what happened until after. Then, after he left, Brad told me Noah was prying for information. He told him that we're roommates. That's how he knew that I would know your info. Please don't be mad."

"I'm going to kill you in your sleep," I shrieked.

"He left right after you did." As if that would make me feel any better!

"Too bad for him; his friend obviously shelled out a pretty penny," I said acidly.

"Stop acting like a bitch! You're obviously upset about this. Talk to me." She pouted her bottom lip.

"I just want to go back to sleep. Can't we talk in the morning?" I begged.

"Fine, but we *are* talking about this. It's like in our unwritten roommate agreement or something like that."

I waited until she shut my door and then I put my face into my pillow and screamed. I tried to sleep but sleep evaded me, and I spent the night tossing and turning.

Sunday morning came with my alarm clock blaring. I hit the snooze button, but it kept roaring through the lousy speaker. Tossing the clock across the room to make it stop, I made a mental note to pick a new one up on my next trip to Target.

I sat up and finally dragged myself out of bed. I went to sit at my desk so I could work on my thesis some more. I opened my laptop, but my mind wasn't in it today. It was in one place. Noah Sinclair… *my drug.* He had officially infiltrated my mind.

Frustrated, I slammed the lid down. *I need coffee.* I huffed my way to the kitchen to make a cup, only to discover we were out. Today was not going to be my day, I could just tell. I went back into my bedroom to get dressed for a Starbucks run and stubbed my toe on the bed frame. *Ouch!*

39

I put on the first clothes I could find - a pair of yoga capris and a zip up hoodie. I slipped on my flip-flops and grabbed my phone from the charger. I backed out of the driveway and headed the three blocks to Starbucks. After standing in line for a good ten minutes, I ordered my venti Bold and headed back to the house in a slightly better mood.

Thankfully, Ellie was still sleeping; she would probably sleep until the late afternoon. *At least I can avoid her inquisition for a couple more hours.* I drank my coffee and was finally able to make some headway on my thesis.

I heard my phone ping. Picking it up, I looked at the screen. It was from a 212 number I didn't recognize.

Jules. Can we do lunch today? Pls. I need to talk to you.

I texted back. I could only assume who it was.

Who is this?

There was a response almost immediately.

It's Noah. Please Jules... I know you don't want to talk to me, but I NEED to talk to you.

Ugh. Why can't he just leave me be? My life has been fine since I let him go and now he has to come charging back in like an angry bull. I texted him back again.

You're engaged. How would your fiancée feel about you texting me?

He finally replied.

I paid Ellie to give it to me. So much has happened and I really need to talk to you. Please, it's just lunch.

Dammit, Ellie. She'd omitted that bit of information last night during our talk. The thought of seeing him again made me feel a whole range of emotions. The fact that I actually *wanted* to see him scared me the most. If there was one thing I knew about Noah, it was that he was relentless when it came to getting his way.

I conceded. **Fine. When. Where. What time?**

I waited for a reply, but it never came. I went back to working on my thesis, but my frustration was really taking me off my game.

About an hour later, there was a knock at the front door. I knew Ellie was still sleeping like the living dead in the next room, so I tore myself away from my computer and went to answer it. There stood Noah, holding a bag of take out. He was in a pair of overly washed denim jeans; a tight fitted gray sweater, and black sneakers. He was looking too good for his own good. I was seething.

How the hell did he know where I lived?

"Hi, Jules." I was furious that he'd showed up uninvited and unannounced. I'd wanted to meet him somewhere neutral. "Can I come in?" he asked, giving me his signature grin.

"No," I said and started to close the door in his face. He put his hand out to stop me. "Since when did you resort to stalking, Noah?" I asked, annoyed.

"Since it involved you." He was being serious. I knew when he was being serious because his brows always furrowed. *Dammit!*

"Ha-ha, you're funny. Seriously? I have a lot of work that I need to do, and you're distracting me."

"Jeez, Jules. Who lit the fuse on your tampon?"

"Listen, Noah, I've had two helpings of flaming bitch this morning. Satan himself wouldn't fuck with me right now. Now, why are you here?" I demanded.

"I told you. I need to talk to you."

"So talk."

42

"If you won't let me come in, can we at least go sit in my car or something?" I clenched my fists and begrudgingly opened the door, allowing him to pass. He smirked, showing off his dimples. *Asshole!*

I gestured to him to sit on the loveseat while I took a seat across from him on the sofa. He looked so big sitting there that I almost wanted to laugh. Almost. He placed the bag of takeout on the coffee table and ran his fingers through his hair. It was a little longer than it had been when we were teenagers. It looked professional.

"All right, you got what you wanted. Now start talking. I actually do have a lot of work to do today," I said.

"What are you working on that's so important?"

"My thesis." I could tell he was trying to distract me. It wasn't going to happen.

"What's it on?"

"Noah," I reprimanded.

"All right, sorry. Um." He absently played with a string on his sweater; he looked nervous. *Good.* "I just want to know what happened after you left. I swear I tried to get in touch with you. Just ask your mom."

43

I winced. "I can't."

"Can't or won't? It was a misunderstanding. She was obviously trying to keep you away from me. I knew she didn't exactly like me, but I didn't think she liked anyone."

"Okay, now that we've cleared that up, you can be on your way. It doesn't change anything. Besides, you're getting married now."

I watched as his face fell. Aren't people supposed to be happy when they're getting married? "It was supposed to be us." He didn't even try and disguise his hurt.

It just brought me back to ten years and a broken promise ago. "You obviously loved her enough to put a ring on her finger. Sound familiar?" I was reminding him of the ring that he had given me.

"Jules, I said I was sorry. Please…"

"Fine. You want the truth? You want the fucking truth? Here's the truth! You got me pregnant!" I screamed at him. "I was so scared. I felt like you abandoned me. My mom found out and she beat the hell out of me. I lost the baby. Are you fucking happy now?"

When I finally gained the courage to look at him, he looked wretched. He actually had tears in his eyes. Seeing him hurt like that killed me. I didn't mean for it to come out like that; it just happened.

"I had no idea. That would never make me happy. How could you even think that about me? Why didn't you call my parents' house? I would have come for you. I told you that before you left." He reached out to me, but I backed away. retracted.

I saw Ellie open her bedroom door and close it quickly. She knew what had happened; she's been there to help me through the aftermath. "It's in the past. I'm stronger now," I told him. "I can take care of myself. I don't need you to ride in on your white horse and take care of me anymore, Noah. I don't need anyone to take care of me!"

"So being a stripper is you taking care of yourself?"

"It pays the bills. It also means that I'm in control. I happen to like what I do."

"The Jules I knew didn't need anyone, either, but I liked that she needed me," he said sadly.

"Noah, you need to go. Go home to your fiancée. I hope you have a good life, but I don't want to see you anymore." I walked to my bedroom, closing the door behind me. I slid down the door and broke into tears.

Chapter Four:
All My Fault

• •

Noah

I hadn't been able to sleep much last night. Jackson practically had to tie me up to keep me from driving to the address Ellie had given me. I still couldn't believe she was here, in New York. It was almost like seeing a ghost. To this day, I still missed her. More than I'd ever admit. She looked incredible, too. She had always been stunning, but she never saw what I saw. Her hair was a lot shorter and she had thin, black streaks throughout. I liked it; it looked edgy. *And her body... Wow!* She was toned and had lost the softness that she had as a teenager. She didn't look hard, and she still had the same killer curves. She was probably pissed about my 'hottie with a million dollar body comment.' I wanted to punch myself!

It was amazing that, even after ten years, she could still knock me on my ass with one look. She was the same sassy, I-don't-take-any-shit, spunky Jules she was in high school. Somehow, though, she seemed more austere than I remembered.

I spent the rest of the night stirring, trying to think of a plan to get her to see me. This morning I was paying for it. To make matters worse, Carrie had decided to ambush my condo first thing, putting me in an even worse mood. Her voice seemed more nasally and irritating than normal. Maybe it was just me.

I felt a shove. "Earth to Noah."

I looked up to see her standing in my face, holding pieces of fabric. Her blonde hair was coiffed into a fancy twist. Her brown eyes were the highlight of her face. Then I had an epiphany. Carrie reminded me of Jules. That's probably what subconsciously drew me to her. *Fuck.* I broke out of my oblivion. "Sorry, what did you say?"

"I asked you what color you thought for the napkins," she snapped.

Shit, we were talking about napkins? "Oh, um, I don't care. Whatever you want," I replied quickly, hoping to avoid an interrogation. I could certainly live without another one of them from her. I had thought I loved her. I tried to love her. She'd pushed the engagement, and I'd finally relented. We were a good match, but

48

looking at her suddenly made me realize that I was probably making a colossal mistake. I needed to clear my head.

"I was thinking champagne colored or maybe chartreuse," she said. I nodded blankly. I wasn't actually hearing anything she was saying. "Noah, is everything okay? Did you do something at your bachelor party that you regret? You can tell me; I'll forgive you," she purred, running her nails up my forearm.

"No, I'm fine. I'm just tired." I stood and walked out of her grasp. "I have some errands to run. I'm going to go shower." I hurried out of the kitchen and into my bedroom.

Closing the door behind me, I went to my dresser. I opened my underwear drawer and reached up to retrieve a picture I'd taped underneath. It was the picture Jules took on our last night together. We had just made love for the first time, and she was kissing my cheek. It was one of my most valued possessions. I used to have it on the end table next to my bed. Carrie had tried throwing it out on more than one occasion, so I hid it. We just didn't have that electricity between us like I always had with Jules.

I've been settling for the occasional spark. I need to find a way to get Jules to talk to me. I needed to know why she'd run out on me like that last night. I had convinced - well, bribed - her friend, Ellie, to give me Jules' contact information. I gave her all the money that the guys had given me for the party; it was over fifteen hundred dollars.

Pulling out the napkin that had Jules' information on it, I started a new text. I hit send and anxiously awaited a response. I started to feel a little guilty, especially with Carrie in the next room, but it wasn't enough to stay away from Jules. She was my kryptonite. She had always been my drug of choice and I needed a fix. I had questions that needed to be answered.

When she texted back agreeing to go to lunch, my heart sped and the anticipation grew. Hopping in the shower, I felt happier than I had been in years. Five minutes later, I was out, and I threw on the first things my hands touched. I didn't even bother to see if they matched. I was officially a man on a mission.

As I walked back into the kitchen, Carrie gave me a death glare. Not in the mood to fight or get stuck, I grabbed my keys and headed out the door with a wave. I sincerely hoped she would be gone by the time I got back. In the past twelve hours, I had gained a lot of perspective. The realization of how unhappy I was with where my life was headed and how I was doing what was expected of me, rather than what I wanted to do. It was a hard pill to swallow and it boiled down to seeing Jules again.

Climbing into my Jeep, I headed over to Happy Wok Chinese to order takeout. I got General Tso's chicken and chicken and broccoli. I hoped they were still her favorites. As much as I wanted to talk to her, I thought it would be more suited for a private conversation. After I paid, I headed toward the address in Amityville that Ellie had given me.

Once I was on my way, I called Jackson. A groggy voice answered after two rings.

"Dude, why you calling so early?"

"Early? It's almost lunch time." I laughed. "I'm on my way to see Jules."

"What? Did I hear that right? I must've misheard. You're crazy. You need to go home to Carrie. This isn't going to end well, bro."What he just said surprised me. He detested her. I'd first met Carrie when I was fresh out of law school, when I started working at her father's law firm. It was the night of a high profile gala that we were all expected to attend. I brought Jackson as my guest, and that's when he started not liking her. Something about her drew me in, though. I realize now that I was trying to make her Jules.

"Bro, you're opening up a can of worms. You should just leave well enough alone."

51

"Dude, unless your name is Google, stop acting like you know everything."

He laughed. "That's funny. I'm definitely using that!" My GPS alerted me that I would arrive in five minutes. I suddenly felt anxious. *What was I supposed to say?*

"I'm almost there. Wish me luck."

"Good luck, fool," he said. "Call me later and let me know how you made out."

I clicked him off the Bluetooth and pulled into the driveway of a little, white house with black shutters. I knew it had to be hers because I recognized the car that she'd gotten into last night when she stormed away from me. The house screamed Jules. She always had a thing for black, white and whimsical. I headed to the black front door with takeout in hand. The walkway was lined with a few fairy gnomes and it made me smile.

Taking a deep breath, I hoped she wasn't going to toss me out on my ass. I knocked quickly before I chickened out. She opened the door and gasped in surprise, then fury flashed across her beautiful face. I was hoping for a better reaction. She had on a cute pair of black framed glasses and her hair was in a messy bun. She was even more beautiful in the daylight, and way better than I remembered.

She tried to slam the door in my face. I held my hand up preventing her from closing it the rest of the way. I was going to make her talk to me. I felt as desperate as I sounded. I knew I shouldn't be here for so many reasons, but there was so much left unsaid.

Finally, she opened the door. I walked past her, not bothering to try and hide my smirk. She pointed for me to take a seat on a tiny loveseat. I placed the takeout on the table before I sat. The room was painted a sage green, and the furniture was oversized black leather. They had a large flat-screen mounted over a brick fireplace. The walls were plastered with tons of black and white pictures of her and Ellie. On the coffee table were a bunch of girly magazines and an arrangement of pink peonies, her favorite. I was surprised to see the décor wasn't overly feminine, like I'd expected. The kitchen was off the living room. It was painted a tomato red with white cabinets and all white appliances.

"All right, you got what you wanted. Now start talking. I really do have a lot of work to do today."

"What are you working on that's so important?" I was trying to start on a neutral subject.

"My thesis." I automatically assumed that she must be in grad school by now. I was proud of her since that's what her original plan was.

"What's it on?" It was my lame attempt to distract her some more.

"Noah." *So much for small talk.* I noticed a pull on my sweater. *I always liked this sweater.* Wow, I'm ADD today... "Sorry." I paused to look at her again. "Um. I just want to know what happened after you left. I swear I tried to get in touch with you. Just ask your mom." It almost looked as if someone had shocked her.

"I can't."

"Can't or won't? It was a misunderstanding. She was obviously trying to keep you away from me. I knew she didn't exactly like me, but I didn't think she liked anyone." Something changed in her face; for a moment she looked horrified. It quickly changed back to anger.

"Now that we've cleared that up," she said, "you can be on your way. It doesn't change anything. Besides, you're getting married now."

I wasn't sure I wanted to get married anymore. I wasn't sure of anything anymore. "It was supposed to be us." I mumbled to myself.

"You obviously loved her enough to put a ring on her finger. Sound familiar?"

I wanted to tell her that Carrie had pressured me into it and that I was too little of a man to tell her no. "Jules, I said I was sorry. Please…" I pleaded. I was hoping to get a glimpse of my Jules. She had built quite the fortress around her in the last ten years.

Her face contorted as she got to her feet. "Fine, you want the truth? You want the fucking truth? Here's the truth! You got me pregnant. I was so scared. I felt like you abandoned me. My mom found out and beat the hell out of me, and I lost the baby. Are you fucking happy now?"

I felt like I had been flayed alive. That was the last thing I was expecting to hear. I was devastated. *A baby? With Jules.* How could something like this happen? Why didn't she tell me? I felt my macho guy façade falter as tears started falling down my face. I reached for her, but she pulled away. "Jules, that would never make me happy. I had no idea. Why didn't you call my parents' house? I would have come for you. I told you that before you left."

She showed no emotion whatsoever.

55

"It's the past. I'm stronger now. I can take care of myself. I don't need you to take care of me anymore, Noah. I don't need anyone to take care of me."

"So being a stripper is you taking care of yourself?" I regretted it as soon as it came out. I was so angry that she kept that from me all these years that it just came out.

"It pays the bills. It also means I'm in control. I happen to like what I do."

"The Jules I knew didn't need anyone, either, but I liked that she needed me."

"Noah, you need to go. Go home to your fiancé. I hope you have a good life, but I don't want to see you anymore." She walked down into a room off the hall and closed the door behind her.

I sat there on the couch and sulked for a couple minutes before Ellie came bouncing out of her room wearing a pair of boy shorts and a tank top. She was short, tan, and had black hair and blue eyes. She was built like a short Barbie, all T&A.

She smiled. "Hey stud, what's all the yelling about?"

"Yeah, sorry about that. I'm gonna go now." I stood up and headed to the door.

"Noah," she called after me.

"Yeah." I turned.

"I'll try to talk to her once she's calmed down a bit. You should know things were *exceedingly* bad after she came here. She's never truly dealt with what happened. I'm not going to say anymore; she'll tell you if she wants to." I knew she was referring to losing the *baby* and God only knows what else.

"Thanks. I think I got you in enough trouble already." I cringed.

"Don't worry about it. I'm a big girl."

I closed the door behind me and climbed into my car. I absentmindedly backed out of her driveway and headed toward the city. In less than twenty-four hours, my world had turned completely upside down. As soon as my brain started working, I called Jackson. I needed someone to vent to, and that obviously couldn't be Carrie.

"Brother-man! How did it go?"

"Not good. Not good at all," I moped.

"Come pick me up. We'll go out for a beer and talk about it like men over whiskey."

"I'll be there in twenty."

57

I hung up and ran through the conversation with Jules again in my mind. I didn't get any answers, just more questions. I wanted nothing more than to turn around, break her door down, and make her talk to me, but I knew she needed time to cool off. I decided that I would give her a week before I tried again.

Fifteen minutes later, I pulled into the parking garage of Jackson's exclusive apartment complex. Just as I was getting ready to shut the car off, 'Don't Go Away' by Buckcherry came on my iPod. The song summed up our situation perfectly.

Jackson and I met on our first day at Fordham University and been friends ever since. He was a trust fund baby and a ladies' man, but he was also funny, loyal, and gave just as much shit as he got. I hadn't been a happy person when we'd met, and he had helped bring me out of my funk. He was the optimist in our friendship.

When he came out the doors of his building, I hopped out of my Jeep.

"Hey, I need to head over to the Duane Reade before we hit the bar." He grinned. "Lexi's coming over later," he said as if it were an explanation. I cocked an eyebrow. "I'm out of rubbers from the last time… We went through the whole box!" I rolled my eyes. He was like a machine; I would know because we'd shared an apartment for two years.

58

We walked into the Duane Reade on the corner, where he picked up his signature black box of Magnums and tossed them on the counter. The emo kid behind the register concealed a yawn as he rang him up. "Fourteen-fifty, please." Jackson handed him a twenty. "Would you like a bag?"

"Nah, she's not that ugly." He grabbed the condoms off the counter and we walked the two blocks to our favorite hangout, Lola's Bar and Grill. We each took a seat at the bar.

The bartender walked over and placed napkins down in front of us. "What can I get you?"

"I'll have a Duval, please, and make sure you put it in the tulip glass." I smacked Jackson on the shoulder because he made it sound so pretentious. I guess it was because it was fourteen dollars a bottle, but still.

"For you, sir?"

"Jack, neat please." I didn't drink that often. Sure, I would have an occasional beer or something, but today called for something stronger. Jack Daniel's was my go-to crisis drink, and all of my friends knew it.

The bartender placed our drinks in front of us and Jackson took a long sip of his hoity beer. "So, what happened when you went there? Was she happier to see you today?"

"No, man. She wasn't. I already told you I asked her to lunch, and she agreed. So I showed up with takeout thinking she would be more comfortable at her own place. As soon as she saw me, she started freaking out. She even tried to shut the door in my face!" He practically spit his beer out and started laughing. "Then she mentioned something that happened after she moved." I cringed, remembering.

"Well, what was the thing that happened after?"

"I got her pregnant."

Jackson choked on his beer and turned bright red. "You guys have a kid? That's why she was so pissed. Oh my God, did you see it?" *I wish that were the case. At least then she would have to talk to me, and she wouldn't be so damn traumatized.*

"No... she lost the baby. She mentioned something about her mom being the reason. I couldn't get it out of her. I'm worried about her, Jax."

"Shit, I'm sorry. I don't even know what to say."

60

"There's nothing to say. I think I'm going to call the engagement off. I need time to process all of this. Besides, if there is any chance that I can have a future with Jules, I have to take it."

Jackson's eyes grew wide. "Robert is going to cut your balls off! You know that, right? He's already shelled out close to a quarter-mil for 'Princess Carrie's' big day."

"I'll give him the money at this point. I don't love her like that. I definitely can't see spending the rest of my life with her. Jules coming back into my life again put a lot of things in perspective."

Not knowing what else to do, he gave me a pat on the back and changed the subject to Lexi, his plaything. She was a voluptuous blonde bombshell, gorgeous in every sense of the word. She was completely smitten and in love with him, but to him it was nothing more than friends-with-benefits sex. We settled our tab and headed back to Jackson's to get my car. I needed to go home and think of a plan how to call things off.

Chapter Five:
I'm Okay, You're Okay

Jules

After Noah left, I climbed into my bed and pulled the covers over me like a cocoon. I mulled over our conversation as tears slid down my cheeks. I'd been four and a half months pregnant when it happened. I hadn't really talked about it since; it hurt too much. The only people that knew were the authorities and Ellie.

My mom was given five years of probation, which was hardly a punishment if you ask me. My dad had a new family in England. He agreed to keep footing the bill for private school as long as I kept my grades up, so I returned there after I was discharged. Thankfully, Ellie's parents graciously welcomed me into their home over holidays and school breaks. I started hitting the gym in an effort to work out my frustrations and I liked the way it made me feel. I felt empowered. I liked what it did for my body, too; the little bit of baby fat I had turned into lean muscle.

Once I turned eighteen, I was cut off financially. Even though I had some scholarship money it wasn't even enough to cover tuition, let alone books or living expenses. I was working odd jobs when one day I was checking out at a local supermarket and was approached by Adam. I thought he was just another sleaze-ball trying to get into my pants. Instead, he gave me a business card and told me to come check out his club. He promised that I could make good money. After a month of busting my ass waitressing and babysitting, it wasn't cutting it anymore. Even worse was that I was exhausted. I didn't have a set schedule, either, so that's when I made my first trip to Double D's. I watched the dancers on stage and felt the music in my veins. Adam offered me a trial and after that first time I was hooked.

In the beginning, I cleared well over a thousand dollars a week just dancing a few days. Soon I had gained regulars and that bumped my average up even higher. I was able to pay for school and living expenses no problem. One of my regulars owned an Infiniti dealership and got me a great price on a brand new Infiniti ILP G convertible that I paid for in cash.

Ellie didn't actually need the money but she started a couple months after me anyway. She was better at it than I was. It was probably because she exuded confidence, and she was a natural born flirt. Pretty soon we saved up enough of a down payment to buy a little, two-bedroom house in nearby Amityville. From the outside, no one would know what we did. I was a student at Columbia, and Ellie was a design major at FIT. My life was exactly where I wanted it to be. Now, Noah comes crashing into me at ninety miles an hour.

Ellie knocked on my door. "Can I come in?" She opened my door, eating what I could only assume was the Chinese food that Noah had brought.

"Sure," I said picking at a piece of invisible lint on my comforter.

"Sorry about this morning. I didn't know he was going to show up like that. So you told him, huh?"

I knew she'd heard most of it; probably most of the neighborhood did, too. "Yeah, I did. I didn't mean to. It just came out."

"Sorry, sweetie. So, what now?" I could tell she was worried about me. She was always worried about me. She always said that friends are the family you choose, and she chose me to be her sister. I loved her for that.

"What do you mean what now? I told him to go have a nice life. I can't do this Ellie…" I started getting emotional again.

She hugged me. "Jules, don't you think you both deserve some closure? After talking to him, I honestly think he wants another chance. He obviously still loves you if he's going through all this trouble."

"He's engaged! I got my closure years ago and I found it myself," I spat.

She rubbed my back soothingly. "Relax. You know better than anyone that making a big life change is scary. But you know what's even scarier? Regret. I think, if you let this opportunity pass you by, you're going regret it. You owe yourself that much."

Getting off the bed, she left me to think. I'd had a few boyfriends over the years, but nothing serious and only Noah and one other fell into that category. It wasn't their fault the rest didn't last. I just knew what I wanted in a partner and my standards were pretty high. When I was a younger, I felt as if someone must have sent him to me. He was my knight, my safe place to fall. I don't even want to think of what my life would have been like without him all those years. Closing my eyes and thinking about the day I met Noah.

I was six, insecure and I had just lost my two front teeth.

66

"Get out! Get out! Get out!" My mom was yelling as she dragged me to the front door by my pigtails. She tossed me out and slammed the door behind me. I don't know what made her so mad. I had just asked her for help with my homework.

I headed over to the giant oak tree in my front yard and sat on the tree swing my dad had made me. I heard the sound of leaves crunching. I turned my head to see where the noise was coming from. The sun was shining on his face. He had dark brown hair and blue eyes with gray flecks. He was beautiful.

"Hi," I shyly swung my feet.

"Hi, I'm Noah Sinclair. We just moved next door."

"My name's Julia, but everyone calls me Jules. Except my mother; she calls me a brat."

"I don't think you're a brat." He was smiling, showing off his new grown-up teeth. "Do you want a push?" I shook my head solemnly. "Are you okay? You look sad." I shook my head again.

He held his hand out, reaching for mine. It felt nice; it was warm and comforting. He pulled me from the swing and we walked to a large weeping willow between our houses. He explained that he had just moved here from Denver. He was nervous about starting a

67

new school, but now he was happy because we would be going to the same school. We became instant best friends.

The years went by and we remained inseparable. Finally during our Sophomore year, he asked me to be his girlfriend. We were perfect together, until we were torn apart.

Part of me always felt like we were meant to be, but I had my heart to think about. I wasn't used to making myself emotionally vulnerable. Then, there was the fact that he was engaged. I didn't want old feelings to surface just to have my heart squashed. A voice in my head screamed, *Maybe Ellie's right!* I wondered if he was happy. He didn't seem like he was, and that made me sad. Maybe we were holding each other back. Maybe we could both get some closure and finally be able to move on.

More silent tears escaped. I wiped my eyes with a tissue and pulled up a new message. I knew that I needed to apologize. I sat there for the longest time, battling with myself on what to say. I picked up my phone and texted him, deciding apologizing was a good start.

Me: Hey. Sorry about earlier, you didn't deserve that.

Noah: No, I didn't, but I understand better now. I also shouldn't have just stopped by. I guess I just thought you'd feel more comfortable at your place. I'm sorry, too.

68

Me: What can I say? I'm stubborn...

Noah: Always were. BTW I'm calling off the engagement. I didn't do it because of you. I just thought you would want to know. I realized that I was doing it for the wrong reasons.

Me: You should be happy, Noah.

Noah: I'm not. I haven't been in a long time. I just didn't have the courage to admit it.

Me: I know the feeling. I had a bit of meltdown after you left...

Noah: Sorry... I wish things were different. I wish you would talk to me, Jules. I have so much I need to say.

Me: I can't. Give me some time...

Noah: As much as you need. You know where to find me.

I dragged my sorry ass through the rest of the day. Surprisingly, I managed to get a lot accomplished. I spent Monday shopping with Ellie and Tuesday, I had lunch with my friend, Chase.

"So, you will never guess who I saw over the weekend," I said, knowing I was going to bring up a sore subject, but he deserved to know.

69

"If I will never guess, then just tell me," he teased.

"Noah."

"As in *your* Noah?" He looked surprised.

"Yes. He came to the club for his bachelor party on Saturday. Then, on Sunday, he showed up at the house." I couldn't tell Chase about losing the baby. He knew I couldn't have kids, but he didn't know why. I didn't want him carrying that around since it wasn't his burden to bear.

"What did you do?" he asked incredulously.

"I tried kicking him out, but he was persistent." I laughed. "We talked a little, and then we fought a little. It's such a mess. I'm so confused. I don't know what to do."

"What does your heart tell you? Be honest and don't worry about hurting me. Just the truth."

"The truth is, part of me will always love him. Just like part of me will always love you. I don't know what I want right now. I just want to finish the semester and start my life with as few complications as possible."

"I need to put this out there," he said, "so you know where I stand. I'm still in love with you, Jules. I know we can't get back

70

together right now, but that's what I hope for. However, I also want you to be happy." That was one of the best things about Chase; he was selfless.

"You're one of the best people I know, Chase. You have helped me more than you will ever know."

We finished our lunch and talked about some more neutral topics. I could tell he was disguising his hurt. I knew what he wanted, but I also knew that I couldn't give it to him. We'd broken things off because he wanted to move back home, and in my opinion, I was damaged-goods. I couldn't give him the family I knew he desperately wanted.

I kissed his cheek and told him I would see him on Thursday. and headed to work.

By Sunday, a week had gone by and I'd heard nothing from Noah. Part of me was relieved since I still didn't know what to do. I wasn't going to make the first move; I knew that much. I threw some laundry in and vacuumed. As I was putting away the laundry, when my phone rang. It was my ex, Reid, who couldn't take a hint. I let it go to voicemail.

I was getting ready to make some lunch when my phone rang again. This time it was Noah. I realized I almost felt giddy; I told myself to calm the fuck down.

71

"Hello."

"Good afternoon, Jules." I laughed. "What are you doing on this fine Sunday?"

"Actually, I was just about to make some lunch. I've been doing some much needed cleaning."

"Why don't you come here for lunch?" he asked. "We can order in. It will be just like old times. We can even watch a movie if you're up for it."

"I don't know if that's such a good idea," I hesitated.

"Listen, it's Sunday. You should be relaxing. Besides, I had a shitty week, and Carrie's a thing of the past. Please? I waited all week to call you. I have literally been pacing a hole in my floor since eight o'clock this morning. Don't make me beg."

"If this is you not begging, I don't want to see the real thing," I joked. "Fine, text me your address and I'll see you in about an hour."

I walked into my bathroom and checked my face in the mirror. My hair and makeup looked acceptable. I *never* left the house without at least applying mascara and lipgloss. I continually applied them throughout the day, like it was second nature. I decided I wasn't getting changed out of my lounge clothes. Sunday was my

72

one day a week to just relax. Besides, he had seen me as I was practically knocking on death's door on more than one occasion. I also didn't want to give him the wrong impression by getting dolled up.

My phone pinged with his address. Plugging it into my GPS, I trudged my way through a shitload of NYC traffic before arriving forty-five minutes later. I looked up as I drove past his building, trying to find the parking garage. It looked like it consisted of fairly new, posh condos. I texted him, letting him know I was there. Sucking in a calming breath, I tried to mentally prepare myself. It's just Noah, your best friend growing up.

I pushed the button for the service elevator leading to the lobby. As soon as I exited, he was standing there wearing a pair of gray lounge pants and a fitted black t-shirt, and I suddenly felt a lot better. *Looks like he still follows 'comfy-Sunday,' too.* He beamed at me as I walked across the marble floor. Leaning in and kissing my cheek, he said, "I'm really glad you came."

"I know," I replied with a smirk.

He pushed the button on the elevator for the twenty-third floor, only two floors from the very top. I hated to think of what would happen if the elevator broke. When we got off the elevator, he ushered me towards corner unit 2301, opening the door into a spectacular open space. There was a living room with a vast picture window that faced the park. The walls were painted a light gray, and the room was filled with sleek, black leather furniture and an impressive media center. Off to the left was a formal dining room with a glass table and seating for eight. The chairs were high-back, black leather, and looked extremely expensive. He had a buffet against the wall with an oversized mirror hanging above it. Off to the right was a state-of-the-art kitchen with black cabinets, dark granite countertops, and all top-of-the-line stainless steel appliances. The walls were all painted different shades of gray. It was masculine, but not what I was expecting. For some reason, I was expecting more of a bachelor pad.

"Nice place," I said, slightly in awe.

"Thanks, I bought it last year. Come on, I'll grab some takeout menus, and you can pick whatever you want."

We walked into the kitchen, and he gave me a handful of menus. I opted to order something from the deli downstairs since it was quick and he said the food was decent.

Twenty-minutes later, the food arrived. We ate at the breakfast bar in the kitchen. It was slightly awkward because I don't think either of us knew what to say. I owed him a face to face apology after how I acted when he came to the house.

I put my hand on top of his. "I'm sorry, Noah." I felt the tears start, but I quickly squelched them. "I feel terrible about last weekend. You deserved to know, but I shouldn't have thrown it at you like that. You got me so angry, and it just came out. None of it was your fault. I don't blame you. I just want you to know that."

"I'm sorry for barging in like that," he said. "I wasn't thinking, either. I just wanted to see you so bad."

"I get it. It's almost like all these years we've gone on with our lives but it was like we were stuck in place. We never got any true closure." My voice broke as I tried really hard to hold back the tears again.

"I completely agree. I've had a lot of clarity the past week." Noah looked hesitantly at me. "Can we talk about it? The baby, I mean."

"Maybe later," I suggested. I wasn't ready to unlatch that box just yet.

He nodded. "Do you want a tour? We can watch a movie, or talk? Whatever you want is fine."

"Sure. You have a breathtaking view." I was slightly envious.

He stood up and offered me his hand. "Follow me." He led me down a long hallway. He pointed out the guest bathroom. It was

75

painted a pale blue with gray and blue tiles and a marble sink. The next room was an office, housing an entire wall of books, a desk, a couch, and a couple of chairs. The next room was his master bedroom, which was about the size of my house. It was painted a darker gray with a white accent wall where the headboard was. I sensed a theme. His bedroom furniture was black. He had a king-sized sleigh bed with white and gray plaid sheets. One side was an entire wall of windows with a balcony. He had two doors on the last wall. One went to a master bathroom suite with a multi-person tub and a separate standing shower with what appeared to be a ton of showerheads. I peeked into the last door. He had a walk-in closet to die for.

"This must have cost a fortune," I stammered, taking it all in.

"I got a good price on it, but it wasn't cheap. I just couldn't give up this view. It was worth every penny. Plus, there's a doorman, a gym, and I have parking, which is at a premium in the city. I don't like not having a car." The way he said it didn't make it sound condescending. Like he was proud of himself, but not boasting.

"I know what you mean. That's why we settled for the outskirts." I laughed.

"I like your place. From what I saw, it's cute."

76

"We bought it a couple years ago. It's in a good neighborhood. It's also far enough away from the city to have some peace and quiet. But we're still close enough for work and fun."

"What do you do for fun?" he asked.

"Well, I've been really busy writing my thesis. That doesn't leave too much free time for things other than work and school right now."

"What's your thesis on again?"

"Romeo and Juliet. Ironic, huh?" I said shyly. *Why am I feeling shy?*

"Very." He smiled and I felt my heart speed up.

"It's about fate and destiny. How Romeo and Juliet scheme to be together, but get caught up in the cosmic warfare of their families. It's about the undeniable power of love, and the downfall of the family. Which is kind of similar to our own story, don't you think?" I asked sadly.

"Did my heart love 'til now? Forswear it, sight! For I ne'er saw true beauty 'til this night," he said in a faux British accent, making me giggle. He reminded me of the Noah I used to know and I started to relax.

"I love that line. Though I didn't take you for much of a Shakespeare fan," I teased, poking him in the ribs.

"That line has never been truer before right now, Jules," he said sincerely. I felt my face heat up. *Dammit, Jules! Get a grip already!*

"Thank you."

"Do you want to watch a movie? Or we could talk…"

"A movie sounds good. I still like to keep Sundays lazy." Growing up, we'd had this thing that, every Sunday, we would hang out together in our pajamas, just eating junk food and being lazy.

"I have *Romeo and Juliet* if you want. Maybe it could help you with the thesis." He smiled. I'd already seen it more times than I would ever admit, but since I wasn't a huge movie person, I agreed.

"Perfect." I followed him back to the living room, where he grabbed the DVD.

"Um, do you mind watching it in the bedroom? The couches aren't as comfortable as they look, plus the sound is better in there."

"I don't know," I said apprehensively. I was worried about falling into old patterns.

"Come on, I promise I'll be a perfect gentleman."

78

I rolled my eyes as he took my hand and led me back to the master bedroom. I took my flip-flops off and climbed onto the bed, grabbing one of the decorative pillows and pulling it to my chest. It smelled like him.

I got comfortable while Noah set the movie up. He climbed in bed next to me and we sat a safe distance apart. I laid my head back as the opening credits started. I don't know what came over me, but I had the sudden urge to reach out and grab his hand or put my head on his shoulder. It was exactly what we'd done when we were kids. I wondered if he was as comfortable as he used to be.

I looked over at him and I could sense he was hesitating, too. We locked eyes and, in that moment, it was like we had never been apart. Ten years, heartbreak, loss, everything was forgotten. We were just Noah and Jules.

We quickly closed the gap between us. He put his hand on my cheek as he guided my face to his until our lips finally met. The same familiar spark ignited; electricity coursed through my veins. I felt alive for the first time in a long time. Noah was my defibrillator. His tongue grazed my bottom lip, and I parted my lips, deepening the kiss. We had both gotten better with age. I pulled away breathless and looked at him.

"I love you, Jules. I always have."

I couldn't doubt his sincerity, but it scared the shit out of me. I was terrified of getting hurt. Someone can only hurt you if you give him that power; I would be giving him the power to destroy me. It was too easy to lose myself with Noah. I needed to stand my ground and put some boundaries out from the start. I don't know that I'd ever stopped loving him. Even when I wanted to hate him I knew I still loved him.

"Noah, I'm not in the market for a relationship right now. Besides, there is still so much we need to talk about. I'm not sure this can go anywhere." I said solemnly.

He cradled my face in his hands. "Please stay with me tonight. We can go to dinner. I'll even sleep on the couch. I just got you back, and I'm not ready for you to go just yet."

"Let's start with dinner, and we'll go from there..." *So much for a lazy Sunday.*

Beaming at me, "excellent."

"I don't have any clothes, so I'll need to run home." I looked down at my loungewear.

"There are a couple boutiques across the street. I'm sure we can find you something acceptable to wear." His lips were still close to mine and his voice was husky with lust. It was taking all of my self-restraint not to pounce on him.

"If you keep that up, we're never going to leave the bedroom."

He sighed. "Fine. Let's go get you some clothes and then we can go to dinner and talk some more."

He changed into a pair of black dress slacks and a light blue button up. I picked up a pair of black Italian loafers and handed them to him. He smiled approvingly and put them on. He grabbed his keys and wallet and pulled me out the door. We walked across the street to Bella's Boutique, where I found a gorgeous, cream-colored wrap dress that I paired with a set of leopard pumps and a thin, brown belt. I could tell Noah loved it by the grin he was sporting. I brought the tags to the register since I was going to wear it out of the store.

"That will be five hundred fifty nine dollars, please," the salesgirl said. I went to hand her my bankcard when Noah pushed my hand away and handed her his black AmEx. *Show off!* I rolled my eyes at him and put my card back in my wallet. I was annoyed, but decided it was better not to argue with him since he was trying so hard.

After we were done, we walked back across the street to the parking garage. He helped me climb into his Jeep, and we headed toward Midtown. He pulled into Per Se, a fancy French restaurant. Amazingly, we were seated right away.

"You look lovely," he said.

"Thank you, and thank you for the dress. You didn't have to do that," I scolded playfully.

"I wanted to. I hope it's the first of many." His response shocked me.

"Noah, where do you see this headed?" I asked seriously.

"To the altar."

"Be serious. We haven't seen each other in almost ten years. A lot's changed since then. We've both changed, a lot."

"I suppose," he admitted. "I think we should start by catching up on what we've missed and go from there. I'm hoping that you'll give me the opportunity to make up for lost time."

"I can't have kids," I said sadly. I knew he'd always wanted kids.

"We'll cross that bridge when we get there. You still need to tell me what actually happened."

I felt the pain in my heart and nodded. He deserved to know. "After we moved here, Abigail wasted no time sending me off to boarding school. I didn't find out I was pregnant until around Christmas break. I didn't say anything to anyone except Ellie. I knew I wanted to keep the baby, since it was part of us. Anyway, when I went home again for spring break, I was noticeably pregnant. Abigail freaked out and called me a whore. She said I probably didn't even know who the father was." I flinched, remembering her wrath. "She ended up getting so angry that she tossed me down a flight of stairs. When I got to the bottom, she repeatedly kicked me in the stomach. I don't remember much after that, except that I lost so much blood I almost died. When I woke up, the nurse said Abigail told them that I fell down the stairs, but they knew that the injuries were far worse than a typical fall. They alerted authorities. Anyway, the doctor told me that, when the placenta detached, it caused irreversible damage. He said my chances of being able to conceive are pretty much nonexistent." I spoke just above a whisper. It hurt so much more to say it out loud.

Noah ran his thumb over my hand reassuringly. He looked as broken as I felt. "I'm so sorry, Jules. I knew she was horrible to you, but I never expected her to do something like that. I wish I could have been there to take you away. I wish you weren't so damn stubborn, and you would have called me. I would have come."

83

"I know you would have. It's the past, though, and I'd rather not talk about it anymore." He nodded in understanding.

The waiter brought out our entrees, and we turned to more neutral subjects and played catch up. Neither of our stories were all that interesting. Turned out he'd graduated from Fordham with a degree in law, which is where he'd met his best friend, Jackson. He was currently practicing law at a large Manhattan firm and looking to become a partner, with Carrie's dad.

When we finished dinner, he paid, and then we headed back to the condo.

"Please stay," he pleaded.

I was surprised that I actually didn't want to leave, either. "Okay," I agreed.

I didn't have class on Monday and Noah had arranged a personal day. I was looking forward to sleeping in and having another lazy day with just the two of us. It would give us a chance to catch up on everything else that we'd missed over the last ten years.

I slipped the dress over my head and folded it neatly before grabbing one of his t-shirts from the drawer and pulling it over my head. We climbed into bed and fell asleep, just like old times. The next morning, I woke up to the sound of high-pitched shrieking. It sounded like a drowning cat. I pulled the pillow over my head to muffle the sound.

"Noah!" the voice shrieked again. "What in the hell is going on here? Who's that?"

I felt him sit up. "Carrie, what are you doing here?"

I turned my head slightly to get a better look at her. She was tall, slender, and blonde. *She looks like a prissy bitch.*

"Daddy said you called in a personal day. I thought we could spend it together. *Obviously,* you had other plans."

I was suddenly anxious. Did he lie to me about breaking off the engagement? I turned to him. He looked seriously pissed off.

"Carrie, go to the kitchen," he ordered sharply. She huffed and spun on her Louboutin's, storming out of the bedroom.

"That's some wakeup call you've got there," I teased.

"I'm so sorry. I didn't think she'd show up like that. I guess it's time to change the locks." He leaned in and kissed me quickly before pulling on a pair on lounge pants and heading to the kitchen. *Damn, he's sexy!* Being the snoop that I am, I went and stood in the doorway to eavesdrop.

85

"Is she who I think she is?" Carrie asked acidly. I wondered how she would know who I was.

"It's Jules," Noah confirmed.

"How long has this been going on?"

"We're not together anymore, Carrie. I'm free to see whomever I choose."

"I'll forgive you this time. Have her leave, and we'll go to breakfast," she said nonchalantly as if she were talking about the weather. *What a crazy bitch!*

"There is no *we* anymore. We've been over this already. It's over. I didn't want this." He gestured between the two of them. "You pressured me into proposing, and I should have never done it. You're going to make some guy real happy one day. I'm just not him."

"You're going to throw everything you've worked so hard for away because of that *slut?* She's so fake, I bet Barbie's jealous!" she scoffed.

"I'd lose everything I have if it meant that I could have a second chance with Jules. Not that it's any of your business, but there's nothing fake on her. Keep your snarky comments to

86

yourself." I loved that he still stuck up for me like he used to. It made me smile.

"This is not over, Noah Sinclair!" she shouted. She was obviously used to getting her way.

I decided it would be easier for him to get rid of her if it looked like we were putting on a united front. I strutted into the kitchen like I owned the place, leaning in and pecking him on the lips. I sauntered to the fridge and opened the door, taking a swig of orange juice straight from the carton.

"You!" She pointed at me with her skeletal finger.

"You do realize it's a finger and not a wand, right? I'm not going to turn into a rat or anything." She did it again, so I did it back. "Abracadabra… nope, you're still a bitch." Noah laughed but quickly covered it up as a cough.

"You are nothing but a no good whore," she yelled.

"For your information, I'm not a whore. I'm a dancer at a high-end gentleman's club. There's a difference. But I bet you're naked under those clothes, you slut." She was shooting daggers at me. I was so full of comebacks, though, that I could've run circles around her. I had dealt with people like her my whole life. Her little digs had no effect on me whatsoever.

87

"Are you really leaving me for this piece of trash?" she still seemed unconvinced.

"She's not trash," Noah said, "and if you say one more thing about her, you're going to find yourself out of here on your ass."

"Wait until Father hears about this!"

Noah grimaced slightly. I'd give her something to stick in her pipe.

"Oh, isn't your dad Robert Collins?" I asked.

"What of it?" Her voice rang with malfeasance.

"Tell him Felony sends her regards. I haven't seen him in a couple weeks," I cooed. Her eyes bugged out of her head. *Checkmate, bitch!* "Why don't you run along now?"

"You're going to pay for this, Noah Sinclair. Mark my words."

She left, slamming the door behind her. Not exactly the morning I'd envisioned.

Chapter Six:
All of Me

●•◦•●•◦•●•◦•●•◦•●•◦•●•◦•●•◦•●•◦•●•◦•●•◦•●•◦•●•◦•●•

"So you still have a thing for blondes?" I teased.

"Only one." He walked across the kitchen and kissed me lightly. I could tell we were both subconsciously falling into our old ways. It was going to have to get nipped in the ass before it got out of control, I wasn't ready to let it happen yet.

"How about I make you breakfast?" he offered. "Then, we can do whatever you want today."

"Sounds good." I replied.

He walked to the fridge and pulled out the ingredients to make cheese omelets and bacon. I got the daunting task of buttering toast. He placed my plate onto the breakfast bar with a smile. It smelled delicious. It wasn't surprising that he could cook, his mom was phenomenal in the kitchen.

When we were finished, he loaded the dishes into the dishwasher and tossed me over his shoulder, carrying me back to the bedroom. He placed me down in the middle of the bed, so I was lying on my back. He leaned over me, supporting his weight on one arm. "I'm going to kiss you now."

Unable to do much else, I nodded. Cradling my head in his hands, he began slowly kissing me. Our tongues danced a slow, magical dance. I ran my hands up and down his sculpted chest, then up his neck and through his hair. *I've missed him.* Even though we had only been together once, nothing was ever able to come close to what we'd had. We had a soul bond.

Scraping my nails down his back, I pulled at his shirt until it was at his shoulders. We broke the kiss just long enough to take it off completely. I took a moment to marvel at his abs, his happy trail, and the V between his hips. His hand slid under my back and up my ribs, trailing his fingertips along my breasts. He pulled my demi bra down and playfully rolled my nipples between his fingers. I stifled a moan. I tossed the shirt I was wearing into the growing pile of clothes.

"Noah... this is no strings attached. Just two friends having casual sex."

"We'll see." He cocked an eyebrow and started kissing me again.

I wanted to say more, but we were all tongues and hands. I kissed down his jaw line to his neck, gliding my hands over his chest down to his happy trail. I found him hard as steel, straining against his lounge pants. Our mouths met again. I stroked him lightly through the thin material swallowing his moans. He unhooked my bra and glided his fingertips down my arms, leaving me topless. He laid me back down and kissed my throat, my breasts, my stomach, before stopping and rolling his tongue around my belly button. He slid his hands under the elastic of my panties.

"Fuck, you're so damn sexy, Jules," he growled.

"You, too," I said breathlessly. I was beyond turned on. Noah's touch sent sensual shockwaves throughout my body and grew with every touch.

He nipped at my hipbones, gently biting down my thighs before resting his head between my legs. His eyes met mine, as he began running his tongue up and down my heat, circling my clit and teasing my entrance. He was good, *really* good. Every lick, flick, swipe brought me closer to the brink and before long I was spiraling.

He sat up with a satisfied look on his face. I returned the favor, taking him inch by glorious inch until he pulled me away. "This is going to be over before we even begin if you keep that up."

Pushing him further onto the bed until he was on his back, I straddled his waist. "I need you," I said, panting as I lined him up. "If you don't want to, now's your chance."

91

He answered by lifting his hips and thrusting into me. It was cosmic, euphoric, astonishing…

"Use my body. Make it yours," he said through clenched teeth. "Oh, fuck!"

He slid out a couple inches and slowly moved in and out, allowing my body to get acclimated. He even hit a sensitive spot I didn't know existed. I interlocked our fingers and used his hands to brace myself. I started moving, up and down, forward and backward, fast and slow, each movement better than the one before. Seeing our connection and how wet I was making him was really turning me on.

"Come on baby, let go. Let me feel you. I can tell you're close," he begged.

He started pumping with a feverish pace, and I let go. The feeling was so magnificent; I felt like I could pass out. He hooked his arms behind my back and switched positions, so I was on my back. He kissed me lovingly as he moved in and out slowly. He was making love to me. I moved my hands to his ass, making him pick up the pace. He kissed my face, my breasts, and my lips, causing a delicious burn. His hair stuck to his forehead. I lifted my hips up to give him a better angle.

"That feels so good," I cried. "Fuck me harder, Noah." He picked up the pace again and I felt the build. I felt him start to

92

thicken. I could tell he was getting close. "Please," I begged. "Come on, Noah, I want to feel you lose control. I want all of you." He let go, and it was beautiful.

He lowered his body onto mine. We looked into each other's eyes, forehead to forehead. He kissed me and cradled me in his arms. I felt so safe with him like this. I suddenly felt vulnerable. "Please don't leave me again." I started to cry. "I need you in my life. It's not the same without you. It hasn't been since."

"Never again. I love you, Jules."

"You too."

I was in such a blissful trance. He picked me up and carried me into the bathroom, sitting me on the sink. As he started to clean me up, we decided to just take a shower. Stepping into the stone shower, I was careful not to wet my hair since it would turn into a frizz ball. He added some shower gel to a washcloth and washed my neck, my back, all the way to my toes, before doing the same to my front. I took the washcloth from him and did the same. When we got out, he wrapped us in a plush, white towel and pulled me close so that we were skin to skin.

Wrapped in a towel, I followed him into the master bedroom and started picking up the clothes that were strewn across the room. Again, everything had changed in a matter of hours. I wasn't sure

93

what to make of it. Part of me was so relieved to have Noah back in my life. The other part was hesitant for fear of my heart breaking all over again. Noah kissing my shoulder broke my thoughts.

"I guess we should probably go out and do something today. Otherwise we're not going to do anything else."

We decided to walk around the city and be touristy for the day. The one clothing store we were in played a Justin Timberlake song and he teased me. "Remember that birthday?" He cringed slightly after he mentioned it.

It wasn't such a pleasant memory for me.

I had just gotten home from school. It was my eleventh birthday, but no one acknowledged it. I didn't expect them to. I was used to it by now. My dad had been transferred to England full-time the year before and he wasn't able to make it home. He would call if he got the chance. My mom was going to dinner with her 'friend' Charles instead, but I was fine with that. I wasn't stupid. I knew Charles was more than a friend. I'd overheard my parents arguing about him on more than one occasion.

Once I was in the safety of my room, I let the tears fall. I went to the kitchen and made myself a macaroni and cheese microwave dinner. I cleaned up the silverware and went back to my room to do some homework. A little while later, Noah had knocked

94

on my window. I always left it unlocked so he could come and go as he pleased. We still saw each other all the time, but he was in high school now, so I didn't see him during the day anymore.

He wished me a happy birthday, and I told him I wasn't in the mood for celebrating. He reached outside the window and pulled a bag inside. He pulled out a small cake. It was a yellow cake with buttercream frosting and strawberry filling… my favorite. He also brought three presents. An N'Sync CD, since I had a ridiculous crush on Justin Timberlake that he always teased me about, a box of Jujubes, since that was his nickname for me, and a picture of us from the amusement park that his mom and dad took us to over the summer. I hugged him gratefully. Sometimes I felt much older than eleven. I thanked him for being my friend. We ate our cake before he headed back home. We knew my mom would be back soon. I fell asleep dreaming about the day I could get out of Greenville, Georgia.

Early that morning, something startled me awake. It was Charles. He was drunk and mumbling something about having a birthday present for me. That sick fuck tried to rape me that night. I somehow managed to fight him off and escape out my window. I ran across the lawn to Noah's window. He opened it up for me and pulled me into his bed, promising to keep me safe. He did, for five years after that.

95

After extensive therapy and realizing that at any time anyone something bad could happen, I was able to overcome that night...for the most part.

"You mean Mrs. Timberlake." I laughed, hoping to lighten the now dim mood.

"Mrs. Sinclair sounds better," he said, feigning hurt.

"Noah, you need to stop with the marriage thing. You've been unengaged for five minutes, and I'm not ready for that kind of commitment right now. We can be friends, but we're going to have to set some boundaries."

"I know. I'm sorry."

Spotting a photo booth across the street, I pulled him in and inserted five dollars. We started off making goofy faces and ended up kissing. We reluctantly dragged ourselves out of the booth before we were arrested for public indecency. We had lunch near Central Park. By the time we were heading back, I was exhausted from all the walking, so he hailed a cab. I knew he was going to try to convince me to stay again, but I had school and work tomorrow. I couldn't miss either. *Though school is closer from here than my house…* I quickly squashed the thought.

"What can I do to convince you to stay?" He pouted.

96

"I need to go home. I have schoolwork to do, and I have to work tomorrow night. I need to get a good night's sleep, and we both know that's not going to happen if I stay here." I knew we would spend the night humping like a couple of horny rabbits.

"What about Wednesday?" he asked.

"School until four and then work from eight to twelve."

"Can I take you to dinner then?"

"Sure," I agreed.

Chapter Seven:
Hands off

•◦•◦•◦•◦•◦•◦•◦•◦•◦•◦•◦•◦•◦•◦•

"Worst day ever!" I whined to Ellie. The phrase *anything that can go wrong, will* came to mind.

"Oh, worse than the time you got pulled over and the cop said 'papers' and you said 'scissors, I win' and he didn't even laugh?" she teased, making me cringe.

"Way worse than that. First, I spilled coffee all over myself, and the car. I even burned my hand to boot. Then, I was so frazzled thinking about everything going on with Noah all day that I couldn't concentrate in class. And the worst of all was when I ran into Reid on my way to the parking lot."

She grimaced. "Oh shit. How'd that go?"

"Not good. He's still not taking it well."

"We're all okay, until the day we're not." *Famous last words…*

"This is my last semester, Ellie. I can't mess up. I think I need to take a step back and reevaluate things."

"I know, sweetie. You'll get there. Reid didn't try anything, did he? 'Cause I will totally go bat shit crazy on him, again!"

Reid Cohen was my last boyfriend. We'd ended things about two months earlier, but he kept finding ways to conveniently *bump* into me. He would basically place himself somewhere he knew I would be. It didn't matter if it was the library or a parking lot; he was there groveling. When we'd first met, I liked how goal-oriented he was, and we'd had a lot of fun together. He was interesting and didn't come off as the clingy type, like a lot of the other guys I met. He was a pre-med student going for orthopedics, like his father. However, although he was attractive and had a decent sense of humor, we lacked that spark. As soon as I realized we weren't compatible, I'd ended things.

He went a little psycho when I told him. He even went as far as saying he was already looking into engagement rings, which shot up a big red flag. Especially since we had only been casually seeing each other for a couple months. I didn't see the sense in dragging things out, with the inevitable lurking around the corner. He felt otherwise and made it known.

100

"No, but he kept trying to convince me to give him another chance. His begging is pathetic."

"Oh boy." She giggled.

I finished applying my makeup and strapped on my signature black stilettos. We were sticking to Nickelback's 'Something in Your Mouth' for the first song and 'Porn Star Dancing' for the second. I effortlessly moved about the stage after Keith announced us. I noticed a special guest front and center in my part of the stage; it was Noah. I wanted to be annoyed, but instead I was slightly flattered.

I decided to give him a run for his money. I shook what my momma didn't give me and worked the pole like a pro. Climbing to the top of the pole, I gracefully hung upside down and lowered myself. We kept eye contact the entire time; it was erotic. With my back to the crowd, I untied my top and tossed it over my shoulder. I was doing my final walk around the stage, collecting my tips, when Noah slid a note into my panties. Preacher gave him a death glare since there was a strict no touch policy. I nodded my head, saying it was okay, and he turned his attention back to the rest of the crowd. I hurried off the stage so I could read it. I practically jumped into my skinny jeans and t-shirt and unfolded the note.

Will you be my girlfriend? Meet me for a drink and give me my answer, sexy girl!

I giggled like a schoolgirl. Did I want this? It was moving too fast, and I knew it, so I would say maybe, with conditions. I quickly took my makeup off and looked over at Ellie. She was reading *Fifty Shades of Grey*, for the fifth time.

"Are you seriously reading that again?" I poked.

"A girl can dream, can't she?" She sighed dramatically. "My new life plan is to stumble into every CEO's office until I find my own Christian Grey."

"Good plan, but if you find him, remember your best friend. I'm going to meet Noah at the bar. Want to join?"

"Maybe in a bit. I'm waiting for Brad." She winked.

"Okay, see you at home then." I packed up my bag and put it by the back door before heading out to the bar. I didn't get two steps into the club before Noah grabbed me from behind.

"Noah," I squealed.

"Who's Noah?" I turned my head and realized it wasn't Noah. It was Reid.

"What are you doing here, Reid?"

"I came to see you. Why else?" This was a new low for him.

"You just saw me earlier. I believe I told you I didn't want to see you anymore," I spat.

"You didn't answer my question," he said angrily. "Who's Noah?"

"That would be me." Noah appeared for real this time. He pulled me to him and wrapped one arm protectively around me. He offered his free hand to Reid. I shrunk into him, getting as close as I could. Reid was sizing him up as if it were a competition. Noah was still clad in his suit, looking like he'd just stepped off a runway. I knew he could throw down if necessary, but I didn't want it to go there. Reid was in a polo shirt, khakis, and brown loafers. He looked like the arrogant ass he was.

"Noah Sinclair," he said confidently. He looked at Reid belligerently. He took his hand and squeezed. "And you are?"

"Reid. Reid Cohen."

"Well, Reid Cohen, Jules is my fiancé. I don't like you sniffing around her work like this, either. So why don't you fuck off and run along, before we have a problem?"

He looked at my hand. "I don't see a ring."

103

"It's at the jeweler being sized," Noah said, without hesitation.

"You didn't tell me you got engaged when I saw you earlier." Reid gave me a contemptuous smile. *Great, he's picking a fight.* I felt Noah tense up beside me and I rubbed his lower back soothingly.

"Actually, that would probably be because I told you I didn't want to see you this morning. Reid, I'm with Noah now. You need to move on."

He reached out in an effort to embrace me, and I shrunk back.

"Keep your hands off my girl or you and I are going to have problems," Noah spat.

"Jules," Reid pleaded. "Why?"

"You need to leave or I'm going to call Preacher, and you'll be escorted out."

"Fine. I'll go, but you'll see you belong to me." He turned and walked away.

I let go of a breath I hadn't even realized I was holding. For being a short confrontation, it was rather worrisome. I breathed a sigh of relief when I saw him walk out the door. Noah placed his hand in mine and led me over to the bar. He sat on a barstool and pulled me to sit on his lap. He ordered us each a Corona and Brad placed them in front of us. I smiled when I noticed he remembered how I liked them. Noah took a long swig.

"Okay, what the hell was that about?" he asked.

"That would be Reid, my ex who doesn't want to be an ex."

"Oh… are there a lot of them that I'm going to have to fend off?"

"It's been over for a couple months now. He's persistent and doesn't think it's over, as you can see. I've made it very clear, on more than one occasion, that there is no chance of us getting back together, but he just won't let it go."

"If he gives you any more trouble, let me know. Jackson and I will take care of it. He won't bother you ever again. Now, let's talk about the answer I'm waiting for." He grinned.

"I still need a little time to think things over. It's not that I don't want to. I do. I just don't see the need to rush anything. But, just so you know, I missed you and I couldn't stop thinking about you all day. I hope that helps your ego, sir."

"Okay, you win this round. You should know that I'm not giving up on us this time. I missed you, too. That's why I'm here."

105

I leaned in and kissed him long and hard until Ellie came up and cleared her throat. I pulled away and gave her a playful, dirty look.

"Take it to the storage closet, you two."

"How about I take you home with me instead?" Noah kissed me again. "My driver's around the block."

Just the thought alone made my whole body grow hot with anticipation. I nodded. He pulled out his phone and told the driver to come pick him up. He'd told me the other day that he usually hired a driver during the week, so he didn't have to worry about traffic or parking.

We were already halfway out the door. "Be safe," Ellie called after us. I pushed him up against the brick wall of the club and started kissing him again fervently. Fuck, he looked so sexy in his suit.

A minute later, the car arrived. The driver came around and opened the door. Thank Heaven for privacy glass. We climbed into the backseat and I quickly straddled his waist, grinding him through the suit material. His eyes looked feral, turning me on even further. He reached into my jeans and moved my panties off to the side. He started slowly caressing me, igniting a smoldering, intense rush. I knew it was going to be steamy.

Ten minutes later, we pulled up in front of his building. I was ready to pounce in the back of the car, but he told me to have patience. I got out first so he that he could strategically place me in front of him. I needed to block his hugely prominent erection. I jokingly whistled on the elevator ride up, rubbing my ass against his front. Once the doors opened, he rushed us inside his condo. He pushed me up against the wall and resumed the kiss. I quickly unbuttoned my pants and pushed them to my feet.

"We're not going to make it to the bed, are we?" I joked, slipping his jacket off his shoulders. We hastily finished undressing one another.

"Not a chance." He lifted me up and wrapped my legs around his waist as he slowly sank into me. I dug my nails into his back and he picked up the pace. I was enjoying the pleasure overload. I looked down, watching him slide in and out. I felt my body tighten, and I knew he felt it, too.

"Come on, baby," he whispered, and I lost myself to him.

I screamed out his name, clenching down on him. "Noah!"

Without breaking our connection, he moved us so my back was on the couch. He continued his expert pursuit until we were both sated. He rested his head on my torso after and I slowly ran my fingers through his hair. I looked over his shoulder; it looked like a tornado ripped through here. I broke into a fit of giggles.

He lifted his head. "What's so funny?"

"Us. We're like a tornado. I think my bra is hanging from your chandelier."

"It looks good there. I think I'll leave it." He smiled, kissing me. "Can you stay tonight? Please."

"Not tonight. I have a long day tomorrow." He pouted his bottom lip adorably. "I'll see you for dinner, right?" I asked.

"I wouldn't miss it. I have a meeting first thing in the morning to discuss things with Robert. The rest of my day is pretty open. At least I don't have to go to court."

"Is everything going to be okay? With work, I mean?" I was concerned that breaking off his engagement with the boss' daughter would cause problems with his job.

"I'm not sure yet. I don't think there is anything to worry about, but Carrie is his little girl, so I'm not sure. It doesn't matter either way." He was holding me as if his next breath depended on it. "I want this to be our second chance, Jules. I won't let anyone or anything stand in the way of that. After spending all those years thinking I would never see you again, I can't go through that again. I won't. So, no matter what happens, as long as I have you, nothing else matters. Besides, if I have to get a new job, I will. You know I don't really need the money."

That was true. When his Grandfather Bill passed away when he was sixteen, he'd left Noah a *very* sizable inheritance. Noah was smart with money so it would be enough to last him the rest of his life and then some.

"I know. I want that, too, but your dream was to become a lawyer. I don't want you to lose that, especially because of me."

"Don't worry your pretty little head."

Chapter Eight: Get Out Alive

●•●•●•●•●•●•●•●•●•●•●•●•●•●•●•●•●•●•●•●

Noah

My alarm went off at six-thirty, just like it did every morning. I geared up for my run and hit the streets of downtown Manhattan. I always ran the same route every day; I had for over a year. Today, though, something was different. I was noticing little things that I usually blocked out or overlooked. For instance, I ran past a couple jogging with a stroller. I wished more than anything that it could be Jules and me one day. I wondered how badly the scarring was, and if there was any kind of procedure available to increase our chances.

Today was also my meeting with Robert. I was hoping that he would go easy on me. I hadn't let Jules know how worried I actually was. When I got back to the condo, I showered and dressed in a navy blue suit. After running some pomade through my hair, I took one last glance in the mirror before heading down to the lobby. Segundo, my driver, was out front waiting for me. I climbed in and tried my best to keep calm. We were about halfway there when my phone vibrated. Looking at the screen, I smiled.

Morning handsome! Thinking of you. Let me know how you make out. <3

Good morning, beautiful girl. I will call you when I'm done. ILU

As we came to a stop in front of the building my anxiety began to skyrocket. I exited the car and headed to the same glass doors I walked through every day. I said good morning to Helen, the receptionist, and wondered if today would be the last time I would do this. It almost felt like an out of body experience. Slowly, I walked to the elevator and headed to the forty-fourth floor. I exited into the offices of Collins, McMillan, Oliver, and Pratt, the place I'd busted my ass to be. The firm boasted a mile long list of high profile clients, which made it a great place to work. Particularly since there was always something going on, and I got to learn all different areas of law.

I strolled towards the back of the building where Robert Collins' personal office was. He was sitting behind his desk, reading a paper and drinking his coffee. I knocked lightly on the doorframe.

"Mr. Sinclair, please come in." He gestured.

Mustering up the bravest face I could manage, I took a seat in one of the brown leather seats in front of his desk. He was a rotund man in his mid-fifties, with salt and pepper hair and rosy cheeks. Needless to say, while Carrie and I had dated, Robert and I had had the opportunity to get to know one another on a more personal basis. That could either hurt or help me right now. He also had a reputation for being merciless and cutthroat in the courtroom. Hence, the main reason I was worried about sitting in this very chair.

"Mr. Collins." I offered my hand, since he was being formal. We shook.

"I'm sure you know why I called this meeting." He looked at me sternly. I nodded. *This is not looking good.* "As you already know, I have put a sizable amount of money towards a wedding that no longer seems to be taking place." He glared at me. "Now there's got to be a reason behind it, so I would like to hear from you why you called it off."

"Sir, if it's about money, I can pay you back, every cent. I'll have it wired directly to wherever you'd like."

"Noah, I'm not worried about the damn money. You had better just hope you have a damn good reason for breaking my little girl's heart." He motioned for me to proceed.

"I can't say you will find it to be a good reason, sir. Here's what happened. While we were at my bachelor party last week, I saw someone I used to know. Actually, not just someone. She was my childhood best friend. Coincidentally, she was also my first girlfriend. We were together for a long time before she was forced to move to New York with her mother. Things happened that were beyond our control, and we lost touch. When I saw her, all those feelings came back, stronger than ever. Carrie doesn't deserve to be hurt while I figure this out. Honestly, this is going to sound harsh, and I don't mean it that way. If Jules would agree to marry me right now, I would book the first flight to Vegas and marry her with no hesitation at all. But we're just taking things slow for now." I sucked in a breath and waited for his reaction.

"I see. So you're leaving my daughter for a stripper." He didn't seem amused, and I could only imagine what Carrie had told him.

"Robert," I started before remembering this was supposed to be a somewhat formal meeting, "Sir, I mean no disrespect, but she only does it to pay for school. She's very intelligent. She said she knew you."

114

I cringed, hoping I hadn't hit a nerve. We didn't talk personal business inside the workplace and mentioning that I knew he frequented Double D's was bound to cross some kind of line.

"What's her name?" he asked, intrigued.

"Julia Kline, but her working name is Felony." I saw his face light up. *Okay, I wasn't expecting that kind of reaction, but it is Jules we're talking about.* I crossed my fingers.

"From Double D's?" He raised an eyebrow.

I nodded. "Yes, sir."

"I've actually had the pleasure of having some conversations with Ms. Kline during some client meetings. She's the whole package. Smart, kind, funny, and stunningly beautiful. Hell, son, if I wasn't already married, I'd want to marry the girl myself and I'm old enough to be her father." He laughed.

"So, you're not mad?" I hesitated.

"I can't say that I'm not disappointed that I won't get you as a son-in-law." I braced myself for what was coming. "But I'm hoping that I can settle for having you as a partner at the firm. You're a damn good lawyer, Noah. You're tenacious, strong-willed, and you remind me of a younger version of myself. I'd hate to lose you to another firm."

115

"What about Carrie?" I asked apprehensively.

"She's my daughter and I love her dearly, but she's a bitch. I know that. Oh boy, do I know it. I think it's partially my fault. I may have over compensated too much... with indulging her, among other things. I wasn't around very much when she was younger. After her mother and I split, she didn't really like wife number two, or three, so she didn't come around much. It didn't help that her mother was on a head-trip. She used Carrie against me in any way possible to get what she wanted. Unfortunately, she was the one to suffer. As I said, I'm disappointed, but I do understand. The heart wants what the heart wants."

I let out the breath that I didn't realize I was holding in and looked at him. He was waiting for me to say something, or did he want to say more?

"Thank you, Robert. I hope that I can continue to learn from you and become a better lawyer."

"About that," he looked at me hesitantly. *Here it comes,* I thought to myself. "I'm thinking we should we change the name to Collins, McMillan, Oliver, Pratt, and Sinclair? That is if you're okay with sticking around?"

"I'd like that very much, sir. I won't let you down."

116

"I know you won't." I stood up and shook his hand. As I was about to exit, he called after me. "All that stuff that I just disclosed doesn't leave this room, understood?"

"Of course."

"Very well. I'll have Mary Beth draw the papers up when she gets in. Why don't you take the rest of the day off and celebrate? I had Nick clear your schedule, in case I needed to fire you." He laughed, but I knew he was serious.

"Thank you again, sir."

I walked out of the room at a little after eight and called Segundo to come pick me up. *Holy shit, I'm glad to have that behind me!* It didn't go how I was planning at all. It went about a thousand times better. I had Segundo stop so I could pick up bagels before we headed to Amityville. I wanted to surprise her since she didn't have class until eleven. At a quarter after nine, we pulled onto the street. I had him stop at the corner so I could call her.

"Hey, sexy," she answered cheerfully.

"Hey." I tried to sound glum.

"Oh no! What happened?" She gasped.

I grabbed the bag and started walking up the street. "He wasn't happy to lose me as a son-in-law."

"Oh, I'm so sorry, Noah." I knocked on the door. "Hold on, someone's here. It's probably UPS for Ellie. I swear she orders more stuff from Amazon than anyone I know."

"Surprise," I said while smiling and holding up bagels.

"You're looking awfully happy for someone who just got fired." She tapped her foot, still holding the phone.

"He didn't fire me. He was disappointed to lose me as a son-in-law, but he hoped I'd settle for being a partner at the firm." She looked completely bewildered. "I accepted."

She squealed and threw her arms and legs around me. "I'm so proud of you, Noah. That's amazing! It's what you've always wanted." I held her tight and consciously sniffed her hair like a weirdo. "It's Philosophy's frosted animal cracker shampoo." She laughed.

When we were teenagers, I used to mow lawns just so I could buy her banana shampoo. It was weird, but I loved the way it made her hair smell. This stuff just wasn't the same. I made a mental note to pick up some banana.

"I like it, but I still like banana better. Now, are we going to eat these bagels? I'm famished." I'd been so nervous this morning that I'd skipped breakfast; now I was starving. I even ate a Taylor ham, egg and cheese sandwich on the way over.

"Yeah, yeah, hand them over." I handed her the bag as she pulled out the bagels and she started putting cream cheese on them.

"So… while I'm here, I wanted to talk to you about something. I was thinking we could go away, maybe next weekend? Jackson's family has a house upstate and I think we could both use a break…"

"I'll have to clear it with Adam and get back to you, but it sounds nice." I walked up to her and lifted her chin so I could kiss her. *I love her so much.* "I thought you were starving."

"I'm hungry for something else right now."

I carried her to what I hoped was her room. Opening the door, I laid her down on the bed. Sliding off her pajama shorts, I dropped down to my knees and kissed my way up her leg until I reached pay dirt. I got to work savoring every inch of her. Our first time she wouldn't let me go down on her and for years I fantasized about what she tasted like. She tasted better than I could have imagined. Shy Jules was gone and in her place was the most incredibly beautiful, sexy woman. Sitting up on her elbows, she

119

lifted her tank top above her head exposing all of herself to me. Gliding two fingers into her heat, I began a slow assault savoring each passing second. I committed each sound and expression into my brain as I watched her unravel. Quickly stripping out of my suit, I positioned myself between her soaking wet pussy and lined myself up. As soon as I was inside her, I was in paradise and she was my heaven. I never wanted it to end. I made love to her, each deliberate movement bringing us both closer to euphoria. Kissing her cheeks, lips, and neck, I was doing my best to make her feel the love I had for her. I held out for as long as I could but when her walls closed down around me I was done. Thrusting into her, I came. Hard.

We finally managed to pry ourselves apart because she needed to get ready for school. I put my suit pants back on and headed to the kitchen to grab our bagels and bring them into her room. When I came back in she was in a pair of leggings, which in my opinion are the bacon of pants, and a pair of knee-high black leather boots. I made a mental note to have her wear them in the bedroom one day.

Wanting to have a few more peaceful minutes before we had to get back to reality, I climbed into bed and motioned for her to join me. We sat in content silence as we ate our bagels. On our way out the door, I kissed her, told her I loved her and that I'd see her at dinner. I was more determined than ever to get her back.

120

Once back in my car, I asked Segundo to take me to the mall so I could do some shopping. There was a really nice, big mall about forty minutes north so we headed there. Even though he was my driver, he was also my friend. I begged him to help, and he begrudgingly agreed. First, I picked up her banana shampoo. Then I decided, since I was already there, that I would pick up a couple necessities for her to leave at my place, for when she stayed. I went to Victoria's Secret; Segundo refused to go in. Not knowing which ones she'd like, I bought every matching bra and panty set I could find in her size.

Next, we headed to Nordstrom. I bought her an entire wardrobe so she wouldn't have any excuse not to stay. I got jeans, t-shirts, hoodies, sweaters, sneakers, boots, heels, sandals, flip-flops, sweatpants, yoga pants, pajama sets, lingerie, a couple dresses, skirts, blouses, and a new Burberry winter coat with a scarf and purse to match. I even picked out an array of cosmetics. I swear the sales lady looked at me like I was insane, and for the total cost, I may as well have been.

I needed to make one more stop before I was done. I headed for Tiffany & Co.

121

Chapter Nine: Butterflies

Jules

"Ms. Kline, please see me after class," Professor Gommerman called as I headed to my seat. He was the professor overseeing my thesis, so I was hoping it wasn't anything miserable like that I was going to have to start from scratch. He was amazing. By far, my favorite professor that I'd had in my entire higher education career. He had been a professor at Columbia for over thirty-five years, yet somehow maintained a relatable, youthful appeal with his students. He was a tall, thin man with white hair and a handlebar moustache; he had a thing for tweed jackets and turtlenecks.

I listened intently throughout the lecture and took notes. When class finished, I took my time packing up my bag and waited for the room to empty before heading down. I stopped at his desk.

"How's your thesis coming along?" he inquired.

"Very well. It's almost done. I'm hoping I'll have a chance to finish it by next weekend."

"Excellent. Listen, that's not why I wanted to see you…" He paused and I saw a worry line crease in his forehead. "I overheard a rumor earlier. Although I'm sure there's no truth to it, I wanted you to be made aware."

"Okay… what is it?" I asked, confused, since all I ever did was come to school, go to class, and go home. Oh and I strip for a living...

"I overheard someone put a complaint into the Dean's office, accusing you of having inappropriate relations with a professor."

What the fuck? "That's preposterous! I'd never do something like that." I was astounded.

"I know, sweetheart. That's why I'm bringing it to your attention. Though your *profession* might cause a problem if it ends up going to a hearing. It may make you look less credible."

"Is there any way to find out who filed the complaint?" I was completely taken aback by the accusation. Who would do something like that? I had a very small group of friends here. I was positive that it wasn't any of them.

"I'll see what I can find out. They usually keep it confidential, except for the boards."

"Thank you, Professor."

"Ms. Kline, you are an excellent student. Please don't let this affect your work."

"I won't," I promised. Whoever did this was just going to make me work that much harder to prove them wrong.

"I'll see you next week. If I hear anything in the meantime, I'll email you."

I could not wrap my head around what just happened. I had no idea who would do something like that. My mind wandered to Reid for a split second, but I didn't think he was that vindictive. Besides, he would be jeopardizing his education career making a claim like that.

I headed to dinner to meet Noah. When I arrived at the restaurant, he was standing off to the side waiting for me. I headed over to him and wrapped my arms tightly around him.

"What's the matter, baby? You look upset," he asked, putting his hand on my cheek.

"It's just something at school. I'll tell you about it over dinner."

"They're setting up our table. It should be ready shortly."

"How was the rest of your day?" I asked and he tried to hide a smile.

"It was fine. I have something to show you at the condo after dinner. You can get ready for work there."

"What did you do?" I teased. I knew that face and it equaled trouble.

"I'm pleading the fifth." He grinned.

We ordered steak, baked potatoes, and broccoli. I told him about what Professor Gommerman had overheard. Noah listened to everything I had to say before he spoke, although he was obviously upset. He started asking me questions that a lawyer would ask a client, which made me laugh, even though I was upset. He promised we would get to the bottom of it.

After we were finished with dinner, I ordered a piece of cheesecake to go. We walked to my car. Since I despised driving in traffic, I tossed Noah the keys. He pulled out and headed towards his condo. He made me promise that I would not get mad at him, no matter what, when we got there. Of course, it made me even more curious as to what he had been doing all day.

"Evening, George," he said to the doorman.

"Mr. Sinclair." George nodded.

Once off the elevator, my nerves were in overdrive. He held the door open. I was relieved when the place looked the same as it had the last time I was here. I noticed two blue boxes from Tiffany & Co. sitting on the breakfast bar. My heart was about to explode out of my chest.

"It's not what you think, I promise," he said. "However, that can be arranged whenever you give me the go ahead." He grinned.

He walked over and picked up the first box, handing it to me. I undid the white ribbon and lifted the lid. *Whew!* At least it wasn't a ring. Inside was a beautiful necklace. It was a key pendant with pink and white diamonds. The charm was a tiny butterfly in platinum and rose gold. It was stunning and probably cost as much as I made in a month.

"I love it. It's beautiful. Thank you."

127

"You're very welcome. Want me to help you put it on?" I lifted it out of the box and handed it to him. He fixed the clasp in place and handed me the other box. I opened it up, and it was an apple key ring with a key attached. "It's a key for here. I want you to be able to come and go as you please. I know you're not ready for anything serious, *yet*. That's fine, but I was sort of hoping that maybe you would consider staying here a couple nights a week. You know, like old times. I sleep better when you're here."

"I don't know what to say…"

"Please tell me you're not mad."

"I'm not mad. Surprised, yes, but not mad."

"Well, that's not all." I cocked an eyebrow. "Please remember you're not mad when I show you the next part."

"This is already too much."

"It's not nearly enough. I love you, Jules. I want you, all of you, forever. I'll wait as long as it takes." He took my hand and led me down the hallway to the master bedroom. When we walked in, I noticed another dresser that hadn't been there the last time. I looked skeptically at him. He nodded for me to proceed.

I opened the first drawer. It was filled with bras and panties of every color, pattern, and style imaginable. The next was filled with pajamas and fitness attire. The bottom two drawers were filled with jeans and t-shirts. He led me over to the closet with his hands covering my eyes. When he pulled away, I noticed he'd sectioned off a portion for me. There were dresses, sweaters, and tops hanging and two rows of shoes. Hanging on the back of the door was a black Burberry toggle coat and scarf. He escorted me out of the closet and into the bathroom. It looked like Sephora threw up in there. On the vanity were rows of different foundations, eye-shadows, blushes, brushes, and lip-glosses. Along with my banana shampoo and other toiletries.

"I even got you pads and tampons. I didn't know which you preferred. They're under the sink," he said proudly.

"I think you thought of everything and then some."

"I just want you to be comfortable here."

"I was already comfortable here. I didn't need all of this." I gestured to my necklace and the dresser. "Noah, it's going to take some time for us to get back to where we were, but as far as I'm concerned, the past is exactly that. We're just going to keep moving forward like we have been. You don't need to make up for anything, but thank you." I kissed him tenderly.

"Does that mean you'll stay sometimes?" He was playing the sad puppy face card.

"I love spending the night with you, and I look forward to doing it more often." I heard him take a breath of relief.

"So will you stay tonight?"

"Noah," I scolded.

"Hey, a guy can dream. Can't he?"

"I'll stay here tonight."

"Oh, I almost forgot I got you one more thing." He handed me a large box off the bed.

"I swear to God if it's a puppy, I am going to commit you." I slowly peeled back the paper. It was the smoked check hobo bag that I'd wanted for the longest time, but was too cheap to buy for myself. "I swear you've always known me better than I know myself."

"I'll take that as you like it."

"I love it."

"Thank God you got over your aversion of accepting gifts," he said.

"Shut up. Now no more buying me things. But, since we're giving out gifts, I may have a present for you, too."

"Oh yeah, what might that be?" He crooked an eyebrow at me.

"Well… I just might share my cheesecake with you." I slid past him and darted towards the kitchen. He chased after me playfully. We leaned against the counter as I fed him the occasional bite. I made sure the last bite ended up on his lips so I could lick it off. I pulled him by his tie and headed back towards the bedroom.

"Does my good boy want shower sex?" I cooed, running my hands through his hair.

He grinned like a kid on Christmas. I slid my leggings down and slowly lifted my top over my head. I stood before him in just my bra and panties, watching him run his eyes greedily over my body. I lifted my hands and deftly undid his tie and unbuttoned his shirt. I got to work undoing his belt as he took off his suit jacket and shirt. I dropped to my knees and took him in my mouth, watching his mouth form an O.

"You are so sexy," he said, his voice raspy.

He pulled me to my feet and bent me over the sink. He unhooked my bra and slid it down my arms, doing the same with my panties. He gently nipped my collarbone with his teeth and ran his tongue up my neck before filling me completely. I was almost there when he pulled out abruptly. I looked at him in the mirror, confused.

131

"I don't like when I can't see your face," he confessed.

Turning, I sat on the sink so he could resume. I could feel his desire as he slowly moved in and out of me, our faces nose to nose. It was enough to send me spiraling into oblivion until he followed. He started the shower and checked the temperature, twice. He washed my hair with banana shampoo as I lathered up a shower puff with some body wash. I rinsed quickly, knowing our little rendezvous was going to end up making me late for work. Walking into the living room, I grabbed my bag of work attire and dressed quickly.

Noah came out of the bedroom and started laughing at me. One look at him and I didn't want to go to work anymore. His body was a paragon of perfection. He was clad in a pair of black boxer briefs with a physique that made him look like a Greek god. I could tell he was baiting me. "You're sure you have to go?" he whispered against my neck.

"Yes. I can't start missing days, *especially* if you want me to get off this weekend."

"I guess I'll just have to call Jackson and see if he wants to come play Xbox with me until you get home." He pouted.

"I'm sorry, baby. I really wish I could stay, but I've got bills to pay." I kissed him lightly. "I should be back a little after midnight.

132

You don't have to wait up for me if you get tired. I know you need to get up early."

"It's fine. I'm usually up until around then anyway. I put you on the list with security this morning, George should still be on shift, but if you have any problems, just call and I'll come right down."

Slipping on my flats, I buttoned my plaid shirt to cover what was underneath and tossed my bag on my shoulder. I grabbed my car keys off the counter which were now attached to Noah's key ring and spun around to him standing only inches from me.

"I love you," he said.

"You, too," I said automatically. I was seriously going to have to tone the love thing down because I didn't want to lead him on, just in case. I knew I loved him, but I wasn't sure what the context was yet. Until we figured it out, I wanted to keep the no strings attached casual sex thing going. It just seemed easier and much less messy. If we ended up together, it would be a bonus.

I arrived at Double D's at 7:54. Thankfully, it took almost no time at all to get there from Noah's. I said a quick hello to Dan, applied some lip-gloss, and changed my shoes to get ready for our introduction. I did it all in just over a minute.

"Where have you been?" Ellie goaded, walking in through the club door before bursting into laughter.

I playfully rolled my eyes at her. "Like you have to ask."

"How are things going with *Noah*?"

"They're good, really good actually. We still have a ways to go and only time will tell, but one day at a time."

"I'm really happy for you. If anyone deserves to be happy, it's you. Noah seems great."

"He is, and the sex is out of this world!"

"I'm jealous. The only sex I'm getting is Brad in the supply closet. He has the tools, but doesn't know how to use them, if you catch my drift." She winked.

I made an all telling face and stifled a giggle. "Too much information."

"You know you love 'em, you know you want to bang 'em. I know I do. Introducing Felony and Miss Demeanor." *He really needs a fresh introduction...* The place was already rowdy.

"Let's get this night over with." We hooked arms and headed out to the stage entry.

134

We started out with our usual routine. There was a rowdy bachelor crowd on my side. Preacher was there, keeping a close eye on them. The tips were fantastic, so I didn't mind. Things were going great until I noticed Reid sitting at the bar. He never came here. He'd scoffed at my 'occupation' when he'd found out what I did. I was more than a little peeved that he showed up two nights in a row, especially because of what went down last night with Noah. I ignored him the rest of my time on stage and hoped he would be gone when we started our next set in an hour.

Ellie and I exited the stage. She went to go do a private dance that I declined for the drunk groom-to-be. I never did private dances. I know it seems kind of hoity coming from an exotic dancer, but they made me uncomfortable. Ellie on the other hand *loved* them. I went into the break room and picked up the book I needed to read for one of my classes and started taking notes. I checked my phone and had two texts from Noah.

Miss you already. Hurry home to me. Jackson's on his way over, but you can call me if you get bored, I'll be waiting. Yours in anticipation.

Is it midnight yet? Jackson's annoying me! You're much better company.

135

I texted him back quickly, so I could get back to my schoolwork.

Miss you, too. Trying to catch up on some school stuff, only three more hours!

The hour flew by in the blink of an eye. Before I knew it, Ellie was back, telling me it was time for us to get lined up again. I can't say I was overly surprised to see both Noah and Jackson sitting front and center when I walked back out. Noah looked slightly embarrassed, like a kid caught with his hand in the cookie jar. I assumed Jackson put him up to coming. I smiled and continued working the stage. A couple of my regulars had come in to boot, making it a great night after all. When I walked off the stage, I saw Noah and Jackson peek through the stage door.

"How much for a private dance?" Jackson asked, earning a smack in the back of the head from Noah.

"Dude! That's my girlfriend. Have some manners." Jackson laughed.

"Girlfriend?" I teased. "I thought you were playing Xbox?"

"Fuck playing Xbox like a couple of teenagers. Why do that when we can see your sexy ass strutting around in almost nothing," Jackson said.

136

"Dude!" Noah scolded.

"Sorry, Jules, but *damn,* your ass is fine!"

"Thanks, Jackson, but my ass is not on the market. I do have a friend I can introduce you to, though."

"Hook a brother up." I stood up and took Noah's hand, heading towards the bar where Ellie would most likely be flirting with Brad. As soon as we rounded the corner, I stopped dead in my tracks. I had been completely sidetracked and forgot Reid was still there. By the time I tried to backpedal, it was too late. Noah had noticed.

"What's he doing here?"

"I have no idea."

He let go of my hand and walked up to Reid. Jackson followed closely behind. "Why the fuck are you here?"

"Hi to you, too, asshole."

"Didn't we just have a conversation last night, fuckwad? Jules is off the market, but even if she wasn't, she is not interested! Now, why the fuck are you here?"

"She won't return any of my calls. This is the only way I can get her to talk to me."

137

"She doesn't return your calls because she doesn't want to talk to you! Ever think of that?"

"I need to talk to her about something I overheard today."

"Yeah and what's that?" I asked.

"Did you cheat on me with Professor Mitchell?" It was the first I'd heard whom I was accused of sleeping with. It could be a significant problem if things went to trial.

"What are you talking about?" I tried to play it off.

"I overheard that you were fucking him the entire time we were together."

"Reid, it's not like that, and you know it."

"It would explain why we never had sex. Not once in three months…"A small crowd was starting to gather.

"I told you I'm not that girl! I've only slept with two people, ever. You already knew that, so why would you even question me?" I asked.

"Look at you, Jules. You work in a strip club for crying out loud! You prance around topless for a fucking living!"

"What the fuck is that supposed to mean?" Noah spat, getting in his face.

"You're a fool! She probably sleeps with a different guy every night," Reid spat back.

Jackson appeared from behind me and punched Reid in the face. "Don't talk about her like that, you pansy-ass piece of shit."

Preacher, the club bouncer, appeared and grabbed Reid by the shirt. He asked what was going on. Noah filled him in, and Preacher happily tossed Reid outside. I was wondering when I was going to be able to catch a break.

The fact that Reid had said it was Professor Mitchell caused me to panic. Noah left me standing there to go have a word with Adam. When he came back, he said Adam agreed to give me the rest of the week, and this weekend, off. I agreed to go to the Richardsons' estate, but firmly stated that I still had to go to school since the semester was wrapping up. At least a break would allow me some time to focus on wrapping up my thesis.

"My family has some connection as Columbia. In fact, my dad is a *very* big benefactor at the university and sits on their board. I'll have him make some calls to see if he can find out anymore about these alleged *allegations.*" He sneered the last word.

139

Ellie ran out from the back and handed me my bag. Noah took my hand and led me to his Jeep with the promise that Jackson would get my car to his place safely. Once we were at the condo, I decided to shower. Noah ordered us some take out, even though I wasn't hungry. I had worked my ass off to get to where I was at school, and only a month shy from graduation, this had to happen and threaten to ruin everything.

I walked into the kitchen and asked Noah if Jackson brought my car back yet. He said Jackson was hanging out with Ellie for a little while. I shrugged my shoulders and went to pick at my chicken quesadilla. Noah sensed my emotional state and pulled me into a hug. I was dreading what I was going to have to tell him. I decided to prolong it a little while longer, just in case it meant the end. Resting my head on his shoulder, I breathed in his scent and it helped calm me. It reminded me of my safe place.

A little while later, we finally headed to bed. Noah said Jackson would leave the keys with the front desk and that I should stop worrying. I curled into him and fell into a troubled sleep.

Chapter Ten: Say You'll Taunt me

Noah

We had just gotten back to my place when my phone rang. It was Jackson.

"Hey man, did you get her car okay?" I asked.

"That's what I'm calling about, dude. Someone slashed *all* her tires."

Thankfully, Jules was in the shower so she couldn't overhear what was going on. She was already enough of a mess after what that asshole Reid had said to her. I wanted nothing more than to break that fucker's pretty-boy face.

"What? How? There's always a guard at the back door."

"Apparently he was *occupied*... if you know what I mean..."

"Can you have Adam check the security footage?" I asked.

"I already did. Dan, *the bodyguard*, was with Carrie. Some guy I couldn't recognize was the one who got the car. He had a hood on and I couldn't make out his face. His build was definitely male, though."

"Are you sure it was her?"

"Positive. What do you want me to do now? Should I call the police?"

"No. I'll handle it on my end. Can you call Segundo and have him get in touch with his cousin in Brooklyn? We need to see about getting new tires on the car by the morning?"

"I'm on it. I'll keep you posted."

I clenched my phone and told myself not to toss it against the wall. *Fan-fucking-tastic... How was I going to explain this to Jules?* I honestly didn't think that Carrie would stoop this low. I knew she was spiteful, but I thought she was classier than this.

When Jules came out of the shower, I lied to her. I told her Jackson was busy hanging out with Ellie. Hopefully my evasion would buy me enough time to get her car fixed. I could tell she was exhausted and more than a little stressed out about the school situation. It killed me to see her like this, knowing there wasn't anything I could do to take her pain away. I made a mental note to call Jackson's dad first thing in the morning. I hoped he would be able to pull some favors and get to the bottom of it so we could put it behind us.

I lifted her off her feet and carried her to the bedroom. I placed her in the middle of the bed and pulled the covers up. "Are you okay?" I asked. This was exactly how she'd looked after we'd found her mom's note telling her they were moving. I was scared of what was going on in that head of hers.

"Yeah."

"We're going to get this all straightened out, okay?" I climbed into bed next to her and tucked her into my side.

"Sure." She shrugged.

"I mean it. I'm not going to stop until this is taken care of. Whoever started this is obviously malicious. They just want to bring you down. Don't sink to their level, baby. Reid's an asshole so don't let anything he said bother you, either."

She smiled and let a small giggle slip past her lips. "I'm not a slut. That's not my thing."

143

"I know, baby. Though you hopped right back in the sack with me," I teased, and she slapped my chest playfully.

"That's because you're *my* Noah. You're my best friend, the love of my life."

I was almost positive she hadn't realized what she'd said. "The love of your life, huh?"

"Did I say that?" She pecked me on the lips. "It doesn't hurt that you're hung like Johnny Sins and you look like an Abercrombie model. I mean, who wouldn't want to spend of her life looking at that?"

"Who's Johnny Sins? Or do I not want to know?"

"He's a porn star." She winked.

"Then I'm glad I fit your standards. Seriously, Jules, you're smart, beautiful, funny and caring. You're also one of the strongest people I know. I would love nothing more than to spend the rest of my life looking at you."

"You never know how strong you are until being strong is the only choice you have."

"I love you."

144

Jules 🖤

The next morning, the alarm went off at six. I decided to get up with Noah so we could go for a run together. It was so odd seeing the city while most of its occupants were still sleeping. It was almost serene for a city that never sleeps. On the way back, we slowed to a jog. Thankfully, we were able to hit Starbucks. I was feeling much more optimistic today.

As we walked into the complex, Noah said good morning to George. I wondered if that poor man ever went home since he was *always* here. Once we were in the condo, we headed to the shower. I could tell Noah was apprehensive about touching me in my current state, but I needed him. I stood on my tippy toes and pressed my lips to his. I slowly grazed my tongue gently over his lower lip and bit down gently.

As soon as I pulled away, it was game on. Hands and tongues were roaming. Pleasure seared through our bodies until we formed our connection. He pinned me up against the shower wall and started thrusting. Still soaking wet, we moved from the shower to the bedroom. By the time we were done, we had been in positions that

145

most people probably only say they know. We could definitely give the Kama Sutra a run for its money.

"That was so hot. I'm surprised we didn't light the room on fire," I joked.

"That just completed my cardio for the day." He leaned in and kissed me passionately.

"Noah, part of me will always love you, and I *love* having sex with you, but I can't give you what you want. If you were to resent me down the road, I wouldn't be able to get past that." I was trying my hardest to keep my heart safe.

"What are you talking about? You are everything I could ever want, and more. I could never resent you. No matter what."

"You want kids," I stated. "I can't have kids, and I refuse to take that away from you."

"First, I would like to examine every option available before we just throw in the towel. One of the attorneys at my firm, Joe, his wife Melissa is a renowned OB/GYN here in the city. Maybe we could make an appointment to see her. We can have her take a look and see what possibilities, if any, exist. If you can't, it's *not* the end of the world. I swear I won't mind. I only wanted kids because I wanted them with you."

146

"We're definitely not there yet, but I guess it couldn't hurt to know what options there are. I still don't want to get either of our hopes up…"

"Jules, my only hope is that you will be mine again one day. I'm hoping that day comes much sooner than later because, as much as I love what we have going on, it would be even better if we were *truly* together. Regardless, I'm so happy to have you back and I love you." He leaned in and kissed my nose.

"I know. You know I love you, too. I'm just not sure if this could work." I gestured between us. "I don't know what to think yet. Part of me wants to, the other part is scared of the what if." Plus, I can't go into a relationship without telling him the truth about Professor Chase Mitchell.

"You can't do anything without risking something. You know that better than anyone."

I nodded my head in agreement.

We re-showered and managed to stay clean this time. He dressed in a pale grey suit, a navy blue button down, a silver tie, and black loafers. He looked devilishly handsome. I went through all the clothes that Noah had purchased and settled on a pair of jeans and a pale, pink blouse. I still had a couple hours to kill before class, so I was going to hang out here until it was time to go. We kissed as I playfully shoved him out the door.

He smirked. "Jackson left your keys at the front desk and Claire at reception knows to give them to you when you go down."

"Thanks for taking care of that." I blew him a kiss and closed the door.

Looking around the apartment, deciding it was definitely time for some breakfast, I went into the kitchen to make some oatmeal with fresh fruit. Sitting on the couch, I was turning on the morning news when I heard the front door open.

"You're back already?" I yelled over my shoulder. I turned and gasped.

"What are you doing here? Where's Noah?"

It was Carrie. She was wearing a trench coat. Her hair and makeup looked like something I would wear to work. *She's probably just wearing lingerie, too.* I could only assume she came here with the hope of seducing Noah.

"I could ask you the same question. If I'm not mistaken, you're no longer engaged. You don't need to keep tabs on him anymore. But if you must know, he had a breakfast meeting." I resumed eating my last bite of oatmeal.

148

"If he's not here, how are you going to get to school?" She cackled maliciously.

"My car, how else?"

"Your car?" She seemed bewildered.

"Yes, my car. You know the thing with four wheels and a steering wheel that goes vroom-vroom. Yeah, that thing."

"I know what a car is, you bitch. I just didn't think *your* car would be going anywhere."

"Why not?"

"I had your tires slashed last night." She said it as if she were talking about the weather.

This bitch is more deranged than I gave her credit for. Wait. She did what? As soon as what she said registered, I jumped up and got in her face. "You did what?"

"You heard me, you whore!"

"What the fuck is your problem?" I looked her over. "Noah didn't want you. Get over yourself."

"You took what I had. You're nothing but a no good whore!"

149

"You have no idea who I am, skank! You know what? You're just pissed because you tried to take a stab at my dignity, but you missed. I've known a million of you. I know all the tricks of the trade. I didn't get this far in life riding coat tails like you. You can't take me on a ride that you can't afford to pay for, bitch."

My little rant was obviously too much for her small brain to comprehend. "Ugh!" She lashed out, reaching for me with her nails, and a catfight ensued.

She grabbed a fistful of hair and started pulling. I pried her fingers loose and used my momentum to toss her to the ground. All those free self-defense classes paid off big time. When I got her other hand free, I pinned them both above her head, and sat on her chest. I was careful not to take part in the attack. I didn't even want to deal with the self-defense mess.

I grabbed my phone off the coffee table and called the police. She spent the time it took for them to get here thrashing and yelling profanities. During this time, her trench coat rode up. I was right. She was wearing slutty panties with no pants. She had the nerve to call me a whore…

When the police arrived, I explained everything that had happened. Since neither of us owned the place, they called Noah. He was already on his way home. One of the cops seemed to be having a hard time not laughing the more I explained. Noah came flying through the door fifteen minutes later.

Running straight to me, he looked at the scratch marks on my arm that Carrie gave me during the scuffle. "Are you okay?"

"I'm fine," I assured him. Carrie was trying to say my injuries were the result of self-defense. "I didn't even touch her. You'd know if I did." I whispered under my breath to Noah.

"You need to press charges." He advised.

Since she didn't have a mark on her, there was no evidence to back up her story that I was the aggressor. Besides, I was here minding my own business when she'd barged in. They couldn't charge her with breaking and entering, since she had a key, but they were slamming her with assault charges. I just hoped it wouldn't cause more issues for him at work.

They arrested Carrie for assault and took her down to the precinct. When things settled down I knew I needed to talk to him about my car. "Noah, did you know about the tires?" I assumed he had, especially since Jackson brought the car back here last night. There was no way he could have driven it with flat tires. *Unless Carrie was lying...*

151

His face grimaced. "Jackson told me last night, but we got new tires put on. With everything you have going on I didn't want you to worry. I was hoping it was just a one-time act of revenge on her part and that you'd never have to find out." I wanted to be mad at him, *I really did,* but I couldn't. In some kind of twisted way, it was sweet.

"Are you sure you're okay?" Noah asked.

"I'm positive. She just caught me off guard."

"I'll call and have the locks changed immediately." He kissed my cheek before walking into the kitchen to call a locksmith. I knew I wasn't going to make it to school on time. I reluctantly opted to miss my first class. I decided to call Ellie and tell her what had happened. She had gone from demure southern belle to ghetto queen in all of five seconds. She was ready to "go beat her mother-fuckin' ass."

A couple minutes later, Noah came back and said the locksmith would be here within the hour. I made us some turkey sandwiches to eat while we waited and finished getting ready for school. I was beyond thankful that I had the rest of the week off. I needed time to process everything that had transpired. Wanting to head upstate earlier than originally planned, Noah was trying to see if he could get the rest of the week off too.

After giving him a quick kiss, I left to collect my keys from Claire. She handed them over with a smile. Once I was in the parking garage and spotted my car, I wanted to go upstairs and smack him around. My car not only had new tires, but it also had new rims. They were black and matched my car. *I wonder if he could help himself.*

I called him and started yelling. He swore it was all Jackson's idea because they didn't have my size tires in stock. They "supposedly" only had this pair of rims that would work. In Jackson's words, "they make it look bad-ass."

I hung up and headed to the university. Walking through the parking lot, I was thankful that Reid wasn't there waiting. I had all the drama I could handle for one day. I headed into the graduate studies department and checked my student mailbox. There were a couple flyers for study groups, a book that my friend Cecile had returned, and an official looking letter. I opened the letter and pulled it out of the envelope.

Ms. Julia J. Kline.
717 Purcell Place
Amityville, NY 11701

NOTICE OF DISIPLINARY MEETING

November 6, 2015

Dear Ms. Kline,

This letter is to inform you that you are hereby required to attend a disciplinary meeting on 11/16/15 at one o'clock in the afternoon. The meeting is to be held at the Center for Graduate Studies in meeting room 4.

During the meeting, the question of disciplinary action against you in accordance with the universities policies disciplinary procedure will be considered with regard to the accusation of inappropriate contact and/or behavior with a faculty member.

The possible consequences arising from this meeting could possibly result in your dismissal from our graduate program.

You are entitled if you wish, to be accompanied by an attorney.

Yours Sincerely,

Albert Chavez

Dean of Graduate Studies

Columbia University

154

Holy Shit! This could not be happening. I reread the letter and pinched myself for good measure. *Yep, it was real...*

I dug through my bag to find my phone, which somehow had managed to make its way to the very bottom. With shaky hands, I dialed Noah. I was trying my hardest not to cry. Crying was for the weak, and I was *not* weak. I walked down the corridor to a quiet corner so I could read him the letter.

"How can they even do this? Don't they need evidence?" I asked. I was feeling the onslaught of a panic attack coming on. That was something I hadn't experienced in years. Life is so much easier when you're anonymous.

"Take a deep breath, baby." I exhaled. "I'm not really sure how these things work. They would need something concrete to base their claim on. I don't think a circumstantial he said/she said accusation going to hold much weight. Personally, I've never had to deal with a case like this before. But we *will* figure it out."

He still wanted to have Randall call and put in a query of his own. He was hoping to gain some more insight into *who* had put in the complaint. Since he got pulled away from their meeting this morning because of the whole Carrie episode, they had rescheduled for tonight to finish. He reassured me over and over that everything would be fine. I wanted to believe him, but I still had to tell him the truth. He promised that he would accompany to the meeting, as my attorney. I hung up the phone and dreaded tonight.

Ahhh! I need to tell him…

Even more horrible was the fact that today was the day I had Professor Mitchell's class. I walked in and took my normal seat in the middle of the lecture hall. I set up my laptop and notebook and settled in. Normally, I found his class to be very engaging, but today I wanted to be as far away from him as possible.

He calmly strolled up the aisle before class started. In barely a whisper I heard, "Julia, please see me after class." I nodded in acknowledgement. We hadn't spoken since we'd gone out to lunch last week.

The next hour was perpetual hell. I couldn't concentrate at all. If I didn't think that this was the safest way to talk to him, I would have feigned being sick and left halfway through. Finally, he wrapped up and I slowly packed up my things, waiting for the door to shut behind the last person before I headed down. When I finally mustered the courage to look at him, I laughed. He looked like a professor today in his khakis and sweater-vest.

"Hi," he said shyly.

"Hi."

"So… I guess you got a letter, too?"

I nodded. "I just got it today. It wasn't me, if that's what you wanted to ask."

"No! I know you wouldn't do something like that. I'm just trying to figure out who would."

"I have no idea, but I should probably get going. We don't need to give them anything else to talk about."

He nodded sadly. Things had been somewhat strained between us since we'd ended things last May. I knew he still harbored strong feelings for me, but it made me uncomfortable. I felt like I was always walking on eggshells because I was constantly worried that I would say or do something to lead him on.

"I miss you, Jules," he whispered. He pushed away from the desk and took a step toward me. I leaned in and stood on my tippy toes, lightly pecking his lips. I couldn't help myself; it was the denouement. I pulled back and put my hand on his statuesque face.

"I miss you, too. It doesn't change anything. Goodbye, Chase." I turned and walked away. I hated seeing him hurt. *Great, how am I going to explain that to Noah?*

I pushed the door open and all but ran to my car with a heavy heart. I knew I wanted to make things work with Noah. That's where my focus was going to stay.

I headed to meet Noah and Randall for dinner at Lola's. I arrived to see them smiling and laughing at a table towards the back. Randall looked like an older, more formal version of Jackson. When I approached the table, they both stood. Randall introduced himself and kissed my hand. Noah kissed my lips and pulled my chair out. I felt remorseful for kissing Chase, even if it was goodbye. They filled me in on what they had discussed before my arrival.

Randall asked me of any possible motive that someone might have. I explained the only people I could think of would have been Reid or Carrie. I told him about the stunt Reid had pulled. Randall said anyone was fair game at this point.

I needed a minute alone with Randall. I didn't want him to embarrass himself by calling the university when the claims weren't entirely false. I asked Noah if he would fetch me a drink from the bar. As soon as I knew he was out of earshot, I took my opportunity.

"I really appreciate what you're doing for me, but before you call, I need to clarify something that I haven't even told Noah yet. I did have a relationship with Chase Mitchell. It was before he was a professor and it ended before school let out last spring. We have conducted nothing more than a teacher-student relationship since before the beginning of the semester."

"How long did the relationship last?"

"For a little over a year and a half. We broke up last May because he wanted to be closer to his family in North Carolina, so he left. He was gone for a couple months, but he ended up getting hired as a professor and came back. We have *not* been romantically involved since. I swear. When I registered for the class the spot just said TBD, to be determined, in the professor slot. I had no idea he was going to be the one teaching it until I got the schedule. I need his class to graduate on time. I want you to know that I work my ass off just as hard, if not harder, for his class as I do any other."

"This could cause a problem if it goes to a hearing. I'll see what I can do. You need to tell Noah." I agreed. I loved that he seemed to be protective of him.

Noah returned with my drink, and I thanked him. Still feeling jittery, it was more enthusiastically than necessary.

Randall said he would put a call in to the dean of the university tomorrow. He promised to keep us abreast. He spoke with Noah a little more about Carrie being a possible suspect. He was a really charming man and had a great sense of humor.

159

When we stood to leave, Randall handed Noah the keys to the estate.

"This set is for you. Feel free to use it whenever you'd like to. I rarely get to make it up there anymore with all of my obligations. It's such a waste to have a beautiful place sit there not being used."

"Thanks, Randall."

We left and headed back to the condo. I was still dreading the talk that I was going to have with Noah when we got home. Parking next to his Jeep, we walked hand in hand as we made our way up to the condo.

There was no time like the present. As soon as we were inside and the door was closed, I sucked in a long breath and crossed my fingers.

"I need to talk to you about something. I think you're going to be upset with me. I want to do it now, in case you want me to leave."

"I never want you to leave." He looked apprehensively at me. "What is it?"

Deciding to just spit it out, "I did have a relationship with Chase Mitchell. The same professor they are accusing me of sleeping with for better grades."

He gaped wordlessly at me; hurt was all over his face. I took a step toward the front door. My greatest fear was now a reality. *I fucked up!* I felt my world crumbling around me. I blinked back the tears that were forcing their way to the surface. I had lost Noah, again…

"Why are you leaving?" he asked.

"I knew this would happen." I couldn't hold the tears back anymore.

He turned me around and clutched me in his arms. "Jules, I'm just shocked, that's all. I wasn't expecting you to tell me that."

He moved us over to the couch. He continued to hold me as I proceeded to explain my relationship with Chase. I explained how I really didn't know he would be the one teaching the class. I told him that, even once I knew he was, I still couldn't drop it since I needed it to graduate. I even told him about the kiss earlier. He looked hurt, but took it at face value. It meant nothing. It was a goodbye, and I just wanted it behind me.

"You know this could complicate things with the hearing, right? I'm sure there are pictures of the two of you. Something like that could be used as evidence."

161

"I know. I'm really sorry, Noah. I wanted to tell you sooner, but I was so worried that I was going to lose you again… My love life has always been a mess. I'm terrible at it."

"You're not terrible at it. You just haven't been with the right person." I knew he was right. When all was said and done, he was the only one. It terrified me. "No more secrets, okay?"

I agreed. He smiled and led me back to the bedroom to start packing for our mini-getaway. I was thankful for my new extensive wardrobe as I loaded up one of his suitcases. We set them by the door and curled up in bed to watch TV. It seemed very domesticated. I turned to look at him and he smiled contently. My heart swelled. The fact that he was still here after everything I made the decision that it was time let him in a little.

I let my wall down. I looked at him and squelched the panic that was bubbling at the surface. "Noah, please don't make me fall for you if you don't plan on catching me."

"I'll always catch you, baby. Always. I wish there was some way I could make you understand how I feel. I give you what you want in the bedroom because I know it's what you think you need, but every time we're together, it's with love. I'm going to earn your love again. You'll see."

His declaration melted me to a puddle of mush. Who couldn't love a guy that said incredibly sweet things like that?

Chapter Eleven: Now or For-Never

·●·●·●·●·●·●·●·●·●·●·●·●·●·●·●·●·●·●·●·

When I woke up the next morning, the bed was empty. I started to freak out, remembering my confession last night. I thought he may have changed his mind, but then I remembered our sweet lovemaking and relaxed. I noticed there was a note on my pillow.

Have a great day! Can't wait to have you all to myself for a couple days…

I Love you ~ Noah

I smiled and practically skipped to the kitchen. I regretted it almost immediately. Sitting like a fixture at the breakfast bar was Jackson. He took one look at me and cocked an eyebrow. "Morning, princess."

Does this place have a revolving door or something? Didn't Noah just have the locks changed?

"Morning… I'll be right back." Since I was only wearing a pair of boy-shorts and a tank top, I scurried back to the bedroom to put some more clothes on. I knew that he'd seen me in less at work, but here, it just felt wrong. I put on a pair of pajama bottoms and walked back to the kitchen.

"I should come here first thing in the morning more often," he teased.

"I should wear clothes more often."

"So, since Noah left already, I figured we could go grab breakfast or something. I figure we should get to know each other better since you're dating my best friend."

"Um, sure, let me go get changed. Again."

I took a good look at what he was wearing so I could dress similar. I didn't want to end up looking like an ass in case we ended up at some country club or something. He had on a pair of jeans, a long sleeved white polo shirt, and sneakers. I headed into the closet and picked out a black sweater, skinny jeans, and knee high black boots. I took a look in the mirror and ran a brush through my hair. I applied a quick coat of mascara and grabbed my new jacket from the closet; it was starting to get really cold in the mornings.

"I'm ready," I said as I returned to the kitchen.

We went to the parking garage and he hit his key fob. *Holy shit!* In front of me was literally the most beautiful car I had ever seen. "What kind of car is that?" I practically drooled.

166

"It's the 2012 Aston Martin Vanquish V12 Black Carbon Edition."

"Okay, whatever all that means. She's sexy. I think I'm in love." I ran my hand along the hood.

"Hey, she's taken," he scolded. He opened the door for me. The inside was just as nice as the outside. The dash looked like something out of a James Bond movie. I wanted one! I kept my mouth shut because I knew if it got back to Noah, he would probably have one parked there when I got home.

"Do not tell Noah I said that."

"Why? Are you afraid of what he'll do if I do?" he asked.

"Yes. You know exactly what he'd do."

"Unfortunately, I do."

He slammed his foot down on the gas pedal, screeching the tires. He adeptly pulled into the morning Manhattan traffic. We headed to the other side of town to a retro diner and ordered breakfast. We talked about our meeting with his dad, sans the Chase part. Then he delved into the tough questions that I would expect from a protective best friend. I tried to explain my reasons for holding back. I told him how I felt about Noah. I said that I was

167

apprehensive because I didn't want us to cling to one another just because we had a past.

"Jules, you know that you and Noah are soul mates. You've known that your whole life. So many people wish they could have the opportunity to have a redo and you're getting that chance."

"I can't have kids."

"And? Noah already told me. You know what he said? He said it doesn't matter and that you're not even sure if you definitely can't. Only time will tell and you don't know what tomorrow will bring." It was quite philosophical coming from him.

When we were done with the heavy talk, he changed to a lighter subject. He went on to tell me about all the things he found confusing about life, which was *a lot.* He told me about his on again, off again thing with a girl named Lexi. He was enjoying sowing his wild oats and wasn't sure he could commit to just her. We started joking around and I liked his carefree attitude. With Jackson, what you saw was what you got.

"Why do you think porn sites have a 'share to Facebook' button? Who watches porn and thinks 'you know who would really like this? My family and friends.' I mean, seriously."

168

I nearly choked on my omelet. "I guess you never know. There might be one that needs sharing." I laughed.

"Did Noah ever tell you about our trip to IKEA when we first got our apartment?" I shook my head no. "Well, I hid in one of the closet unit thingys and walked out saying 'I'm from Narnia.' Then, there was this other time I got *really* drunk at a party and harassed some kid with glasses and an accent because I thought he was Harry Potter. Who does that?" He scratched his head as if he were remembering.

Jackson was certainly amusing, and I could tell why he clicked with Noah. He would actually be perfect for Ellie. "Jackson, you should ask Ellie out. I swear you guys would be like two peas in a pod."

"Yeah? Maybe I'll ask her out sometime. So, tell me about this *professor.*" I cringed. I swear boys gossip worse than girls!

"I'm sure you already know his name. Chase Mitchell. We met during my sophomore year at Columbia. He was a doctoral student at the time. He was really good looking and we just kind of clicked. We dated for almost two years. By then, he had graduated and wanted to be closer to his family. His dad got really sick, so we decided to part ways. There were no hard feelings. We kept in touch and he visited a couple times. I honestly had no idea he was planning

169

on coming back. He said he got the job right before the semester started. At the time, we didn't know he would be my professor, but our relationship ended a long time ago."

"So, I don't need to worry about you hurting Noah?" he asked.

"Absolutely not," I said vehemently.

"But you kissed Chase, yeah?" *Ugh! Damn Noah...*

"It was a goodbye kiss, nothing more!"

"No need to get all defensive, princess. I'm just stating the facts."

"Sorry, I guess I'm just on edge lately. Things between Chase and I are in the past, and that is exactly where they are staying," I said firmly.

"Glad to hear it. Are you excited to go upstate later? It's a nice place."

"I'm looking forward to getting away for a bit," I admitted. "It will be nice to have some alone time with Noah."

"Indeed." He cocked an eyebrow. I felt my face heat up. I could only imagine what other personal information Noah allowed Jackson to be privy to.

Jackson paid for breakfast and offered to let me drive home. I practically tackled him for the keys.

Carrie

"I have to take this," I said to my dad. He had come down to the police station to straighten out the charges that stupid whore pressed.

I answered my phone. "Is it taken care of?" I asked.

"I'm working on it. She got the letter from the dean today. Are you sure this is what you want? It could end up backfiring on both of us."

"Oh, I'm sure. I want Noah Sinclair, and I always get what I want." My plan was brilliant. Luckily, I got a certain someone who wanted her just as much as I did to take the bait. Everyone had a price.

Noah

I walked out of the courtroom with a triumphant victory under my belt. Pulling my phone from my suit pocket, I dialed Jules and hoped she was faring okay after spending the morning with Jackson. He had a tendency for being all over the place and saying whatever popped into his head. I always told him that his brain to mouth filter was missing.

Walking out the revolving doors, I started making my back to the office. She answered on the third ring. "Hey, baby. I'm all done with court, but I have to go back to the office quick and to do some paperwork. I'll be home in an hour or so. Do you want me to stop for anything before I get home?" I asked. I had driven to work today so I could stop and fill my gas tank before we left for upstate.

"I'm good. I'm actually out with Jackson right now. He let me drive his car!"

"Wow! He must really like you; no one drives his car." I laughed.

"I guess we'll head back now," she said.

"See you soon." I hung up the phone and ran across the street when the light changed. I quickly finished filing the proper papers and headed home.

Pulling into the condo, I parked next to Jackson's Aston. I shook my head, thinking about how Jules probably wanted one now. Taking my briefcase out of the trunk I walked to the front of the building. I winked at Claire, the receptionist. She was old enough to be my grandmother. I knew she loved it, so I always indulged her.

I was getting impatient waiting for the elevator and almost opted for the stairs when the doors finally opened. When I walked in the door, I was surprised to see Ellie there, too. I thought I heard laughing. I quickly realized it Jules, crying hysterically. She was clinging to Jackson for dear life. As soon as I processed the scene, I rushed to her. I wanted to scold him for not calling me. Knowing Jules, she probably convinced him not to because she hated interfering with my work.

"What happened?" I asked. She let go of Jackson as soon as she saw me. I kneeled in front of her and wrapped my arms around her. She shook her head, letting me know that she couldn't speak just yet.

I looked at Jackson. He should have called me regardless of what she said. "Don't look at me like that. She got a phone call right

173

after we got back. Whoever it was upset her. She started crying like this." He gestured to her. "I told her I was going to call you and she freaked out, so I called Ellie."

I scooped her up in my arms and carried her to the bedroom, leaving Jackson and Ellie behind. I placed her on the bed and took my jacket off, lying down next to her. She pressed her face into my neck.

"Shhh. Every thing's okay, Jules. I'm here," I whispered into her hair.

"No, it's not." She choked and handed me her phone. "She found me."

She pulled up a voicemail, and I pressed play to listen. "Well, well, you can't even answer the phone for your own mother. How long has it been, you little slut? I heard your whoring around has caused even more problems, as if it should come as a surprise. No one will ever want you for anything other than that Julia, *ever*." The message ended. I had to refrain from calling that bitch back and giving her a piece of my mind. I knew that the façade Jules kept up of being tough as nails was faltering before me. She was breaking.

"I don't know how she found me, Noah. How does she know what's going on?" She sobbed.

174

"I don't know, baby. We'll figure it out. Let's get you cleaned up and ready to leave." I helped her into the bathroom and wiped the smeared mascara off her tearstained face. She asked me if she could be alone for a minute, and I reluctantly agreed.

"I'm going to go talk to Jackson and Ellie," I told her. I walked into the living room and told them about the message. I thought Ellie was going to explode; she was so angry. She went on a wild tangent about how she couldn't understand how a mother could act like that. I knew that Abigail Kline was an ice queen. For as long as I could remember, she treated Jules more like a nuisance than a child.

"Jackson can you call your Uncle Ethan?" He was an ex-FBI agent, turned private investigator, and he had an office here in the city. I wanted him to do some digging, call in some favors, whatever he had to so we could shed some light onto the situation.

Jackson put him on speaker and explained what happened. Ethan promised he would do what he could. He said that he was going to look into Chase as well. Jackson was going to go lend a hand, and Ellie agreed to help, too. I thanked both of them and went to get Jules. They yelled a good-bye to Jules and headed out the door.

175

After checking to make sure that everything was ready for our getaway, I hoped it would be a good distraction for her, especially with all the drama surrounding us. I held her hand as I carried our bags down to the Jeep. Opening her door, I helped her in and started toward the thruway.

She was very quiet for most of the trip. I didn't want to press her since I knew she was trying to think things through in her head. I knew she would talk when she was ready. I also knew that Abigail got to her. When we were about three-quarters of the way there, she looked blankly out the window and spoke. "She's right, you know."

"What do you mean? You are *not* a whore, Jules. She's a spiteful bitch! She has done *nothing* but use you as a pawn your entire life!"

"No, I'm not. But she's right that no one is ever going to want me for just me. They're just going to want me for my body. Even look at us," she said.

"That's not true. I like your body, but I love you. You have my heart in the palm of your hand. What you do with it is up to you, but it beats for you. I would like to remind you that *you're* the one who wanted to keep it casual. If I had any say in it, we would be on a plane to Vegas right now. I mean it," I told her.

176

"And what about all my hold ups? I'm just like her. I'm selfish. I come with enough baggage to fill a U-Haul, I can't have kids, and my life's ambition is to write for *Rolling Stone*. You have your shit together, Noah. You're a lawyer. You come from a normal family. You're everything I'm not," she said sadly.

"You are the most unselfish person I know. They say opposites attract, but I think you forget how much we have in common. I don't know how many times I have to tell you the baby thing isn't a deal breaker. We'll go see Melissa when we get back or maybe I can convince them to come up over the weekend. Either way, I want *you*! What can I do to make you see that?" I asked.

She started crying and I wanted to punch myself for pushing her when she was already upset. Then something occurred to me. It was a missing piece to the puzzle. I remembered when I went to visit her after she moved. It was during spring break. Her school was closed for breaks and holidays and students had to go home. I wanted to surprise her since every time I'd tried calling her, it was like my number was blocked. When I showed up, Abigail told me she was away with a new boyfriend. She had probably still been in the hospital, recovering from losing *our* baby. Needless to say, when I'd left, I was devastated beyond comprehension. I had specifically chosen Fordham University just so I could be closer to her.

177

I hated Abigail more than ever now, but I needed to snap Jules out of her self-loathing. "Do you love me, Jules? I mean really love me?" I asked.

"I think I do, but I don't know if I'm confusing my feelings. I'm scared, Noah."

"Without over thinking it, what does your heart tell you?"

"That I love you," she whispered.

"Then take the gloves off and quit fighting it. Just let it happen. Let me in," I pleaded. "I had no idea what actually happened when I came to visit you. I do now. She told me you were away on spring break with a new boyfriend. I was devastated. Honestly, I didn't date for a long time after I found out. Ask Jackson. I was a recluse when I started school. Eventually, even when I started dating again, I felt the same way you do right now. I was scared shitless. I had a couple girlfriends before Carrie, but nothing serious. I forced myself to move on, and it fucking killed me. Carrie had to push me for a long time to marry her. I relented because I thought it was the next step. I almost made the biggest mistake of my life. I never thought there was a possibility of *us* again. I figured you had moved on with your life without me and that I should do the same. I thought you would probably be married or something by now, because any man lucky enough to have you should know enough to cherish you."

"Thank you."

"It's always been you, Jules. Since I was eight years old and I saw you on that damn swing. You've managed to overcome so much, and you had to do it mostly on your own. I'm sorry for that, but I'm here now," I told her. "I shouldn't have given up so easily, but I want a second chance to prove to you that we belong together. I love you."

She started crying harder. I remembered that day like it was yesterday, the day my life changed forever. The day I met my little blonde haired angel.

"I'll try," she said, "but you're probably going to regret it. Especially since the hearing hasn't even happened yet. There's a possibility it could land in the press. If they connect us, it could be detrimental for your career."

"Let me worry about my career and you focus on getting through the end of the semester. I'll make sure everything is okay," I vowed.

"You always do."

The GPS announced our arrival as I pulled up to the gate and pressed in the code. The gates opened and we headed down the tree-lined drive up to a massive stone house.

179

Chapter Twelve:
Leave. Me. Alone.

Jules

We pulled up to a massive stone house. Noah grabbed our bags from the trunk, and we headed to the front door. The entranceway showcased an expansive foyer with a grand double staircase and corridors on either side. The entire house was incredible. There was no doubt that all the furniture was imported. The place was immaculate.

After a quick tour of the house, we made our way upstairs to check out the bedrooms. We decided to take one on the second floor with a great view of the sweeping backyard. The walls were painted a cranberry red. A king-sized brass bed covered in cream and gold linens was the focal point of the room. I started opening doors. The first was a walk in closet and the second was to the en suite. It boasted a two-person tub, a stand up shower, and a double sink.

Noah dropped our bags at the foot of the bed and we set out to explore the rest of the house. There was a library, a billiard room, a media room, eight bedrooms plus a master suite, four additional bathrooms, an eat-in kitchen, a dining room, sitting room, and living room. The fridge and pantry had been stocked for our arrival.

In awe of everything I became even more curious about the Richardson's and their money.

"Noah, what does Randall do for a living?" He laughed and looked at me funny. "What? I'm serious."

"He owns Richardson Communications. They own a bunch of media outlets, but they've expanded and have their hands in a lot of different pots now."

I felt slightly stupid for not putting two and two together. It also explained why Jackson didn't really work, even though he'd graduated from Fordham with a degree in engineering. It also explained his Aston.

"Actually the other night at dinner, Randall asked me to take over the legal side of Richardson the other night. I meant to tell you, but with everything going on it slipped my mind and didn't seem like a big deal."

182

"Not a big deal!" I screeched. "Noah, that's huge! That's an amazing opportunity to show what you're made of and he obviously thinks very highly of you."

He shrugged as he pulled some shrimp cocktail from the fridge to snack on. I started to prepare our eggplant gratin and decided here was a good place to talk a little more about our 'relationship.' Deep down, I knew he was still my Noah, but a lot changed in ten years. I didn't want to pick up broken pieces anymore. I wasn't sure my heart could handle losing him again.

Trying my best to put everything involving Reid or my mom out of my head I focused on Noah. As if he sensed my anxiety, he pulled out chocolate mousse. Swiping his finger in the bowl, he ran it along my neck, following with his tongue. It was a pleasant distraction. I decided to play a little, too. Dipping my finger in the dish, I smeared some on his lips, licking it off seductively. I tried to pull away, but he crashed his lips to mine.

"You and I are going to set this room on fire," he growled.

He reached out and pulled my shirt over my head, trailing his hands south. He kneeled in front of me as he unbuttoned my jeans, peeling them off slowly. Standing to kiss me, I grabbed the front of his shirt, ripping it open and scattering buttons across the floor. Making quick work of the rest of our clothes, he sat me on the

183

counter. His tongue roamed my body, making me wild with anticipation. Lowering my hand, I stroked his impressive length. I love how he felt in my hand. When I turned my head, I was met with a pair of adoration filled blue eyes. I remembered our conversation on the way up here. He was *my* Noah, and I needed to let him in the rest of the way, or I would lose him. It was quite the realization. I felt my apprehension disintegrate with each passing moment. *Holy shit! I love him… really, truly love him!*

"I love you, Noah," I panted.

He entered me swiftly, filling me. "I love you too, baby, so much."

He wrapped my legs securely around him, and without breaking our connection, carried me to the bedroom. Lying me on the bed, he continued to rock in and out. Sitting up on my elbows, I watched our connection, my juices coating him. Each move brought me closer to an orgasm. As much as I loved slow, loving Noah, I needed him to pick up the pace.

"Fuck me. Hard. Please." I begged in his ear.

He didn't need any more guidance as he reared back and slammed into me. Within seconds my was freefalling into bliss. My body practically shaking from the aftermath. He followed and pulled me next to him. With my head on his shoulder, it was perfect.

We stayed there until I saw the time and forgot that dinner was in the oven. Grabbing a t-shirt out of Noah's bag, I hurried down the stairs. Seeing the clothes strewn across the kitchen, I couldn't help but laugh. Luckily dinner was safe and not burnt to a crisp. I got us each a plate and poured two glasses of wine.

"So, I was thinking maybe after dinner we could call Joe and speak with Melissa. I know she's very busy, but I'm sure she'd be able to squeeze you in."

Dread blanketed me again. I knew kids were important to him and this could be a deal breaker, so the sooner we got it over with the better.

We sat in front of the fire with our glasses of wine as Noah dialed Joe. We gave her a brief overview of my history and possible infertility situation. She happily agreed to take me on as a patient and even offered to come up since she had a friend from medical school that had a practice not far from where we were staying. Both nervous and excited we agreed and they said they'd be up sometime Friday afternoon.

When we woke the next morning, I sat up and stretched my deliciously sore muscles. Noah looked at me with adoration like he always did. I leaned in and kissed him before taking off in a run

185

toward the bathroom, only to have him toss me over his shoulder and place me in the shower.

Once we were dressed, we decided to head into town and do some exploring. We window-shopped and admired the quaint little stores. I had to drag him away from the pet store when he tried to convince me to get a puppy. We indulged in waffles that were out of this world. After he paid for breakfast, he told me he needed to make a couple calls. He felt guilty, so he suggested I get a pedicure to pass the time. We headed down the street to the spa. As soon as I was comfy, he went outside. I relaxed in the chair and reflected on the past twenty-four hours.

Noah came back in while later, I was sitting at the dry-bar where my nails were curing. He said they hadn't been able to find out anything concrete yet. I started asking my own questions, which he circumvented. *Typical lawyer.*

Once she was all situated, and I knew I had a little while, I excused myself to call Jackson. I wanted to see what he'd found out, if anything.

"Hey," he answered on the first ring.

"Any news?"

"Nothing affirmative yet. It seems the little bit of info she offered on Mitchell checks out. He's twenty-nine. He just moved back from North Carolina. It's his first year as a professor. He has two brothers and a sister. No spouse or known girlfriends could be found. She said he was good looking, but damn, even I think he's hot." He laughed. "I mean, he's *really* good looking…"

"Jackson," I scolded.

"Sorry. Anyway, we're working on getting the cell phone records for her mom and Carrie. I already looked through hers and his number doesn't show up once. I erased all of their emails from the school server and blocked his number. I went to Double D's and had Adam pull up the footage from the night he was there and wiped that, too. Adam knows if anyone asks, he's to say the system was down for an upgrade. As far as I'm concerned, I don't even know why the school is bothering. There's no evidence that would point to inappropriate contact," he said.

"What do you mean the night he was there? When was he there?" I was greeted with silence. "Jackson, I hear you breathing."

"Dude, don't get your panties in a twist. It was over a month ago. Ellie told me to check the cameras because she remembered him coming in. He was there with a group of friends. She had one drink with him and left."

"Sorry. Keep up the good work and let me know what else you find out," I told him.

"Will do."

I ended the call and started compartmentalizing what he'd just told me. I tried to compile a list of possible suspects. There was Reid, Carrie, Abigail, and now possibly Chase. I wasn't going to leave any stone unturned. As I paced up and down the sidewalk, something caught my eye. I made one last call to a local airfield and made arrangements for a hot air balloon ride.

Heading back inside the spa, I went to Jules. She looked up and smiled brightly. I told her I'd spoken with Jackson, but that we hadn't heard anything new. I paid for her pedicure and led her back to the Jeep.

We headed to the outskirts of town. When I pulled into the airfield, I could tell she was excited. I wondered if she would be as excited if she knew what I was planning. I walked around and opened her door. We walked hand-in-hand to the middle of the field where we met Charlie, the hot air balloon operator who would to take us up.

I helped her in, and we started to rise. The view was spectacular. Once I had her attention, I reached in my pocket and pulled out a ring box. I lifted her hand and kissed it lightly. "I love you, Jules. Ten years ago, I made you a promise. I promised that I would be with you, wherever you were. I wasn't able to keep it then, but I plan on keeping it now. I know you're not ready to get engaged. *Yet.* I'm hoping I can change your mind, but for now, I want to set up a list of new promises. I promise to be what you need, when you need it. I promise to take care of you and always consider your feelings. I promise to love you, and only you, until I take my last breath. This is our second chance," I said.

Her eyes brimmed with tears as she looked at the ring. I could sense a little apprehension, but she nodded in understanding. I carefully slid it onto her ring finger. It was an infinity band of white gold surrounded by diamonds. I liked that it was impressive without being gaudy. It glimmered in the sunlight, which was exactly why it had caught my eye at the antique shop in town.

"I was going to get you a Ring Pop, but I figured it would get too sticky," I joked. Come on, Jules… say something.

189

She reached out and hugged me. *She was speechless.* It was yet to be determined if it was a good thing or a bad thing. Charlie told her that I was a keeper. I leaned in and kissed her.

"I finally know what it's like to let someone in, and that's because of you. But you know I can't marry you… I'm still holding out for Justin Timberlake," she teased.

"I hate to break it to you, baby, but I think he's already married. I hope one day you'll settle for being Mrs. Sinclair instead."

"What? How could he do that to me?"

I wrapped her in my arms as we took in the breathtaking view before our descent. When we got back to the house, she said she wanted to work on her thesis for a little while so I decided to sit in the living room and watch some shows. A little while later, she brought me my laptop, and she handed me a CD, along with a couple papers. I unfolded them. It was a note with some scribbled lyrics. I put the CD in my disc drive and pressed play.

Noah,

These songs explain my feelings better than I ever could.

Love, Jules

190

Noah's playlist:

Lifehouse - First Time

My Darkest Days - Can't Forget You

Ever since we were little, Jules was always better expressing herself on paper. She would always write me little notes or make me mixed tapes before CDs were around. I knew what she was trying to say. She didn't want to get hurt again, but she didn't want to live without me. *What a relief!*

Jules

Time was flying in our paradise bubble and before I knew it Friday was here. Noah planned a really lovely day. We had massages and lunch at The Overlook. He was attentive as always. I was a little nervous about meeting Melissa later that night. When we arrived back to the house, we only had a short amount of time before our company was supposed to arrive. Knowing what my previous doctors had told me, I was already expecting the worst. The optimist in me, though, said maybe there could be a procedure to reduce

191

scarring and increase our chances. However, I was still apprehensive.

I opened up my laptop and checked my email quickly. There were a couple new ones. The first was from Ellie.

From: Ellie Townsend miss_demeanor@doubleds.com

To: Jules Kline felony4u@doubleds.com

Miss You!

Friday, 2015 Nov 30   6:38pm

Hey Sweet Cheeks,

I'm so bored and lonely without you! I'm busy helping Jackson when I'm not at work. I think Jackson and I may have solved our life's problems. We are going to try the casual sex thing, too, since it worked so well for you and Noah (we already did it, *twice*, and holy shit!!!) I'll give you all the details when you get back…

We decided that we don't have to like each other's friends (he likes you, though). We don't have to deal with family drama (so

192

far, his family is awesome), and we especially don't have to date. It's perfect!

We haven't been able to find out too much more. It would appear that Abigail moved again since the last time you and I checked, but we're still looking.

Miss you like crazy!

Xoxo,

Ellie Mae

From: Jules Kline felony4u@doubleds.com

To: Ellie Townsend miss_demeanor@doubleds.com

I MISS YOU, TOO!

Friday, 2015 Nov 30   7:17pm

Ellie Mae,

I miss you, too. Noah and I are having a good time, though. You have to have Jackson bring you up here sometime. It's stunning!

193

I told him the other day that the two of you would be perfect for each other.

We're having company tonight. It's this attorney that Noah works with and his wife, the OB. I'm scared shitless... I'll let you know how I make out. See you Sunday!

Kisses,

J

The next email was one I was not expecting. In fact, I wanted to delete it before even reading it. Nothing good could come from this...

From: Chase Mitchell <u>CMitchell@gmail.com</u>

To: Julia Kline <u>JKline@gmail.com</u>

Read in private.

Friday, 2015 Nov 30   10:22am

Jules,

194

I know this probably isn't the smartest thing for me to be doing, but I don't have any other way of talking to you. Did you have my number blocked?

Anyway... I wanted to let you know, under the advice of my attorney I put in my resignation. I agreed to take a polygraph test, which is scheduled for tomorrow morning. It should clear you of any wrongdoing and allow you to graduate on time.

I have decided to stay in New York a while longer anyway. I was hoping maybe we could meet for a drink sometime. I really do miss you and don't like how we left things. I'll forever regret losing you.

Yours,

Chase

From: Julia Kline JKline@gmail.com

To: Chase Mitchell CMitchell@gmail.com

Re: Read in private.

Friday, 2015 Nov 30   7:23pm

Hey,

No, I didn't have your number blocked. What happened when you tried to call?

I hope you didn't resign just because of me. We would have figured a way to work it out. I'm actually away until Sunday night. I'm not sure that meeting for a drink is such a good idea…

I shouldn't have kissed you the other day. It doesn't change anything between us, Chase. Remember when I told you I ran into Noah a couple weeks ago? We're trying to work things out. I owe it to him to give him all of me. We're going to see where this goes, but I don't see it ending. I'm sorry.

Jules

I got a response almost immediately.

From: Chase Mitchell CMitchell@gmail.com

To: Julia Kline JKline@gmail.com

Re: Re: Read in private.

Friday, 2015 Nov 30   7:29pm

You're still worth fighting for Jules. I'll be waiting in hopes that I get a second chance…

I'm still in love with you.

Chase

To: Chase Mitchell CMitchell@gmail.com

From: Julia Kline JKline@gmail.com

Re: Re: Re: Read in private.

Friday, 2015 Nov 30   7:31pm

Chase, I'm taking this love off life support. I owe it to both myself and Noah to give this a fair try. Sorry, J

There was a knock. I turned to see Noah standing in the doorway staring at me curiously. "Hey baby, everything okay?" he asked.

197

"I'm great. Actually, I was just about to head downstairs."

Closing my laptop, I pulled him into a hug. Standing on my tippy toes, I gave him a quick peck on the lips before taking off on foot down the long corridor. He playfully chased after me as we ran around in circles, until he hopped over the one couch and caught me by my waist, pulling me on top of him to pick up where we left off.

"I love you so much, Jules." He started tickling me.

"Love you too, Noah," I squealed as the doorbell chimed.

He climbed off the couch and promised we would pick up later. I quickly fixed myself, hoping I looked presentable as Joe and Melissa walked into the room. She was tall and slender with reddish-blonde hair and a smattering of freckles across the bridge of her nose. I noticed her bright green eyes when she smiled brightly at me. Joe was about the same height with blonde hair, brown eyes, and a sun-kissed tan.

Noah put his arm around my waist and gave introductions. "Joe. Melissa. I'd like you to meet my girlfriend, Jules."

"Pleasure to meet you, Jules," Joe said taking my hand and shaking lightly.

"Nice to meet you," Melissa said. She had a warm and pleasant aura, and I liked her already.

198

"I'm glad to finally get to meet you both as well. Thank you for taking the drive," I said sincerely.

"It's no problem. Thank you for having us. We're always looking for quick escapes from the city."

Noah and Joe took the luggage to one of the spare rooms while Melissa and I headed to the kitchen. I poured us each a glass of white wine, and we took seats at the kitchen island.

"So, how did you and Noah meet?" she asked.

"Actually, I've known him for most of my life." I laughed. "He moved next door to me when I was six, and we were instant best friends. We lost touch for a few years, but I'm glad we found each other again."

She smiled. "I'm glad to see Carrie gone. I didn't like her. I don't care if she was the boss's daughter or not. She rubbed me the wrong way." I snorted. "Noah said you wanted to talk to me about some things… we could talk later if you want."

"Now is fine," I said. "I'm not sure where to start, so I guess I'll just start at the beginning." She nodded for me to proceed. "Noah was my first. We only slept together one time, right before my mom moved us to New York. She threw me in boarding school the first chance she got, and that's when I found out I was pregnant. I was

199

scared because I didn't think Noah wanted anything to do with me anymore. It turns out now that it was all a huge misunderstanding. Anyway, when I was home for spring break, I was noticeably pregnant, and my mom freaked out. The trauma I suffered made me lose the baby. The doctors said the scarring is pretty bad, and my chances of conceiving are pretty much nonexistent." I wanted to give her as much information as possible while sparing her the gory details.

"I'm sorry you had to suffer through something like that, especially at such a young age." She placed her hand on top of mine and rubbed it reassuringly. "I've arranged for us to go to my friend, Laura's office tomorrow. I'll take a look there and let you know what I can see. When we're back in the city, I would like to run some other tests at my office."

"Thank you, Melissa. It means a lot to Noah and me. I don't want to get either of our hopes up. But knowing he wants kids I just want to know what the chances are, if any."

Joe and Noah joined us a little while later. We talked and laughed most of the night. I really liked the both of them and could tell Joe and Noah had a good relationship by their friendly banter. It was late when everyone headed to bed. I was a bundle of nerves waiting for what my visit with Melissa held.

200

The next morning, I awoke and tried to keep optimistic. Noah seemed to be in a good mood. We'd had a little tiff last night when I convinced him to go to a football game at a local university while I went with Melissa. He kept trying to protest, but I objected and he dropped it.

I showered quickly and headed down to the kitchen. Making a cup of coffee, I tried to play it cool in front of the others.

Noah kissed me passionately and wished me luck. " No matter what the news is, I love you and we'll get through it together."

"I love you, too."

I followed Melissa to her white Range Rover and got inside. *Every thing's going to be fine.* I chanted it over and over in my head.

"I met Laura in med school and we ended up doing our rotations together. She moved up here to start her own practice a few years ago. I figured this was an opportunity for me to get to see her and help you at the same time."

"We, I, really appreciate you helping. This has been a struggle for me for a long time and I would really love to give Noah the family I know he wants. I want it too, but in order to keep myself sane and from getting heartbroken I don't like to get my hopes up."

201

We drove for about forty minutes before pulling up in front of a small, blue house with white shutters. There was a black and white sign out front that read, *Dr. Laura Chamborg, OB/GYN.*

Climbing out of the Range Rover, I took a steady stream of deep, calming breaths. Following closely behind Melissa, who was trying her best to be reassuring, we pulled open the white door and walked in. The room was a pale pink and housed a receptionist desk along with a row of chairs. I noticed a toy section in the corner.

"May I help you?" the receptionist asked politely.

"Yes. I'm here to see Laura, she's expecting me," Melissa said.

"One moment. I'll let her know you're here. Can I have your name?" she asked.

"Melissa McMillan."

The receptionist stood and walked down a narrow hallway to the end, where Laura's office must have been. A couple moments later, a willowy brunette came out to meet us. The first thing I noticed was she had a warm smile and was naturally very pretty. She didn't have on any makeup. She definitely didn't need any, either. She and Melissa greeted one another and then Melissa introduced me.

202

"Follow me back here," Laura said. "You can use room 4. It's the largest and houses all of my equipment." She smiled.

I nervously placed one foot in front of another until we reached the room. She opened the door and showed us in. It was painted a pale cream and was filled with an array of state-of-the-art equipment. I noticed a table with stirrups and an ultrasound machine.

Melissa handed me a gown and stepped into the hallway. *Here goes nothing.* I changed quickly and sat on the edge of the exam table. My heart was beating frantically while I waited. Finally, she opened the door. I noticed she had changed into a pair of maroon scrubs.

"All right, Jules, first things first. I'm going to take a couple vials of blood to send to the lab. Then we will do an internal exam along with a few other tests. Is that okay?" she asked.

I nodded. She walked over and started drawing the blood. When she finished, she helped me lie back and then she started her exam. I thought about how my own mother had possibly ruined my chance at motherhood. It was ironic. Then I turned my thoughts to Noah. Suddenly, the thought of Chase and his recent emails crept its way in. Why now? Everything in my life was just about where I wanted it. He had to choose now to complicate things? Part of me

203

knew I would always love Chase, since he had helped me heal in more ways than he would ever know. But...

I thought about a lot of things. Anything to distract me from what was going on. I tried to lie still as Melissa poked and prodded. *Everything happens for a reason*, I told myself. When Melissa was done, she looked at me. "I want to run some more tests when we get back to the city, but from what I can see, the scarring is pretty extreme. It doesn't look good." She sounded solemn. "I don't want to give up just yet, though."

My heart shattered into millions of tiny pieces. I know I'd told myself I wouldn't get my hopes up, but apparently they had been higher than I'd thought.

"Thanks for doing this for me," I said, trying my best to hold my tears at bay. I was sinking and struggling with myself. I could feel the loss of what could never be. Melissa patted my hand reassuringly and left so I could get dressed.

I put my "big girl panties" on and slapped on a brave face before heading into the hallway. We thanked Laura and went to get something to eat. Ten minutes later, we pulled into Ella's Eatery. I didn't think I could stomach food, but I knew I was hungry. I ordered a Panini and some soup; Melissa ordered the same. We talked at length about what she'd seen, and I tried to listen. She told me she also suffered from fertility issues and had miscarried twice. It didn't make me feel better, though. I felt guilty. I didn't want to take fatherhood away from Noah, despite what he'd said.

I paid for lunch since she had gone through the trouble to try and help, and we headed back. She didn't pry as we drove to the Richardson Estate. I politely excused myself when we arrived and headed to our bedroom to ran a bath. When I was finally submerged, I let the tears flow freely. I hated my mother more than anything.

I don't know how long I was in there before Noah walked in. He placed his hand in mine. It broke my heart, and it was my fault. He dipped his hand into the water.

"The water is freezing," he said. "Your teeth are chattering." He hurriedly walked over to the sink and grabbed the towel I'd left sitting there. He helped me stand and wrapped it around my shoulders. Drying me off methodically, he led me back to the bedroom. He quickly stripped out of his clothes and pulled us under the duvet. "The body heat will help raise your temperature faster," he explained.

Once my body temperature was back to normal, he helped me into my pajamas and wrapped me back in the duvet. He pulled me close, running his fingertips up and down my arm. I knew he knew.

"Did you talk to Melissa?" I asked sadly.

"I did." He paused and kissed my lips lightly. "I'm sorry, Jules. I'm so sorry. It doesn't change how I feel about you. You're what I want. Nothing will change that." I knew it came from the heart so I let it be for now. "We're going to take this one day at a time. Melissa said there might be some different options that she's not familiar with that could help. She wants to discuss it with one of her colleagues and we will take it from there. I love you." He kissed my temple.

"I love you too, Noah." I closed my eyes.

The next morning, I woke with Noah holding me tightly. I moved so I could take a long look at his strikingly handsome face. I decided that there *had* to be some reason fate had brought us back together. The fact that I couldn't give him a baby someday was still weighing heavily, though. If it truly didn't matter to him, maybe with time, it would heal in me, too.

"Morning, gorgeous." He smiled.

"Morning."

"There's my girl. Feeling better today?" He sounded concerned.

"A little." I tried to be reassuring. "I don't know if I will ever be able to get past it completely, but for now, I just want to live in the present."

"I'm glad. I promise it will all be worth it in the end. We should pack up and head downstairs. If we don't leave within the hour, we are going to get stuck in a ton of traffic."

I stood up and stretched. I picked some comfortable clothes to wear for the ride home and packed everything else in my suitcase. He lifted our luggage and rolled it downstairs, leaving it by the front door. We walked into the kitchen and greeted an exceptionally cheerful Joe and Melissa. They were laughing and smiling at one another. Noah ran this thumb over my knuckles and smiled. It was exactly what I needed.

"Good morning, you two," Joe said enthusiastically.

"Morning," Noah and I said at the same time.

We stood around the kitchen island and talked for a little while before heading back to the city to beat rush hour. I hugged Melissa and thanked her again. She told me she would make a follow-up appointment next week to finish her exam.

The ride back was quiet, but it wasn't an uncomfortable silence. I was deep in thought when Noah said something that I didn't quite catch. He snapped me from my trance. "Jules, did you hear what I said?" he asked.

"Huh? Sorry, I was daydreaming." I laughed.

"I asked if you were okay staying at my place tonight. This weekend was emotional for both of us. I just want to hold you close."

"Yeah, that's fine. I have work tomorrow anyway." Satisfied, he held my hand a little tighter.

A few hours later, he smoothly pulled into the parking garage and into his assigned spot. He snatched up our luggage and led me to the lobby. Once inside the condo, I put my bag in the bedroom and headed to the kitchen to make us something to eat. I was going to have to make a point to go grocery shopping tomorrow.

I decided to make us some fettuccine Alfredo, since it was quick and easy. Noah seemed very pleased since he oohed and ahhed over the entire meal. When we were finished, he loaded the dishwasher and called snuggle time. It was exactly what I needed; I was still emotionally worn out after yesterday. Exhausted, I ended up drifting to sleep sometime after ten. I woke up thirsty a little after one and went to the kitchen to get a glass of water.

I was leaning against the refrigerator drinking when I saw Noah's phone flash, indicating there was a new message. I decided not to be nosy since it was probably just Jackson. When it went off again, though, I peeked at the screen. My anger flared. It was a text from Carrie.

I really need to talk to you. I know you said we could meet on Wednesday, but it's imperative, and I seriously need to talk to you before then. Please call me in the morning.

I wondered what she needed to talk to him about and why he hadn't mentioned it earlier. I climbed back in bed and spent the rest of the night tossing and turning. Noah got up at six in the morning as always, but I opted to stay in bed. I hadn't slept well.

He came back a little while later from his run. I heard him in the shower and vaguely remembered him kissing my forehead before leaving for work. I finally woke up a little after nine, a little more refreshed. I showered and dressed in a pair of jeans and a chunky, soft sweater with the plan of going shopping. I fired up my laptop and checked my emails before heading to the store. There was one from Chase. There were no words, just an attachment. I clicked on it.

It opened to a picture of Noah and Carrie, time and date stamped this morning. They were embracing and it looked like more than a friendly greeting. My stomach turned. I wondered what was

209

so important that she was sending him messages at one in the morning and demanding a meeting. Then I started to feel childish. I was more secure in our relationship than this, right?

I picked up my phone to call Chase and noticed a couple missed texts from Noah.

Good morning, beautiful. Have a fantastic day!

Hey, let's meet for dinner tonight @ Lola's. Say 6?

Something just felt off. There was no I love you, I noticed…

I scrolled through my contacts until I got to Chase and hit send.

"Hey, Jules," he answered on the first ring.

"Hey, Chase."

"I'm assuming you got my email. Listen I don't want to meddle in your business or anything, but it just looked and seemed downright suspicious. He seemed annoyed at first, but then his whole demeanor changed. I just don't want to see you hurt again."

"I know. Thanks, Chase. So have you decided what you're doing yet? Are you staying in the city still or are you headed home?" I asked.

"I haven't made up my mind yet. I think I'm going to head home for a couple weeks and figure things out. I'll let you know."

"'Kay." There was an awkward silence.

"I love you, Jules," he said.

"I know, Chase. It still doesn't change anything, though."

"I'm here if you need me."

"I'll talk to you later," I said.

I hung up the phone. Part of me wanted to go home and go back to bed. I decided to put off groceries and head to the library at school to do some research instead. I had barely gotten anything done over the weekend. I packed up my things and headed down to the garage. After I climbed into my car, I stared at myself in the mirror. I had a sinking feeling that something was wrong.

I pulled into school and went to check my mail. There was a letter from Dean Chavez saying there was no longer an issue with Professor Mitchell. He had resigned and passed a polygraph. At least one thing is going right, I thought.

I spent the entire day in the library wrapping up my thesis. When I checked the time, I was surprised it was already after five-thirty. I was so happy that it was the last week of classes until finals. Then I was done. Finished. Free. I was packing up my bag when my phone rang.

"Hey, baby," Noah said.

"Hey, I was just getting ready to leave."

"Can we reschedule?" he asked. "Something urgent just came up, and I have to take care of it. Sorry. I'll try and stop by later and see you in between sets, okay?"

"Sure. I hope everything's all right."

"Everything's going to be fine." I don't know who he was trying to convince.

"All right, see you later then." Then he was gone. Again, no goodbye, no I love you, nothing.

Chapter Thirteen: And the Cradle Will Fall

———•—•—•—•—•—•—•—•—•—•—•—•—•—•—•—•—

We will face it together.

I woke up in a cold sweat remembering the conversation that Noah and I had had earlier. Over the past few days, it seemed like Noah had been avoiding me. It was very uncharacteristic for him. I tried to write it off as it being work-related, but I wasn't convinced. Ellie claimed she didn't know anything. I figured she would know if something was off, especially since she and Jackson were officially an item now.

Finally, Noah showed up at my door first thing in the morning. I was more than a little annoyed with him and his recent behavior.

"Hey," he said shyly.

"Hi, Noah." I didn't even attempt to hide the bitter edge in my voice.

"Can I come in?"

213

I wanted to let him stew, but I also wanted to know what the fuck was going on. Reluctantly, I opened the door the rest of the way. He walked in and I noticed he didn't even bother taking off his jacket. *That's never a good sign.* I went into the kitchen and started making a pot of coffee. He followed me and took a seat at the table.

"Sorry about this week. I was trying to work through some stuff."

"And shutting me out," I spat.

"Listen, Jules… we have to talk about something. It's *big*. But I want you to promise me you will listen to everything I have to say before you start in, okay?" I nodded hesitantly. "It's about Carrie." He paused, watching for my reaction. I remained stoic. "She's pregnant."

It felt as if someone had reached into my chest and squeezed my heart, crushing it. I heard him call out my name, but I wasn't hearing anything. He tried to take a step toward me. I held my hand up telling him to stay where he was. I felt my world crumble.

"We will face this together," he said.

I took a moment to let it sink in. I knew what I needed to do. It was as much for him as it was for me. "Are you fucking kidding me, Noah? You expect us to face this together? You got the girl you were supposed to marry pregnant, and you expect *us* to face this together? Have you lost your fucking mind?"

"Jules," he cried, reaching for me again. I stepped back out of his reach.

"I'm not mad at you, Noah. I'm happy that you are going to have the opportunity to be a father. It's what you wanted all along. Since it wasn't in the cards for me to give that to you, I'm glad. You know I'm not a bitter person. I'm certainly not Carrie's biggest fan, but I wish you both the best." I felt the tears brim over and fall onto my cheeks.

He reached out, and I didn't fight him this time. I didn't have the strength. Besides, I found solace in his touch. "I love *you,* Jules." Tears fell down his face. "You're the one I want to be with. Do you have any idea what this has been like this week? I want to do this together." He wrapped me tighter in his arms.

"Do you think Carrie would ever let that happen?" I asked. He shook his head no. "I love you too, but you deserve a family. I can't give that to you. I will *always* love you. I know what love is thanks to you, but I can't take this away from you. You need to go find her and let her know."

I found my strength and pulled away from his embrace. I went to my room and left him standing distraught in the kitchen. I

215

allowed myself to grieve. I mourned the loss of what we had and what we could have been. When I was finished, old Jules was back with a vengeance. I didn't need anyone to take care of me; I wasn't that girl. I wasn't the one to let anything hold me down. I was, however, the girl who picked herself up and dusted herself off.

I turned my iPod dock up as loud as it would go and blasted 'Thrash Unreal' by Against Me! Other than the junkie part, the song pretty much has me pegged. I was going to keep on doing what I needed to get by.

I could never manage to leave the past far enough behind. To make matters worse, I was starting finals today and I certainly didn't need this. I decided I was placing it out of my mind for the rest of the day. I was ready to start living, once and for all.

I fixed my coffee in a to-go cup and noticed there was a note from Noah on the counter. I picked it up, stuffed it in my bag, and headed to school. I knocked on Professor Gommerman's door to hand in my thesis.

"Come in," he called. I opened the door and walked into his office, which was the size of a closet. Tons of books lined the wall and his desk dominated the small space. "Miss Kline." He beamed. "I'm looking forward to reading your thesis."

216

I handed over the thick binder. I was proud of it and the irony of my topic wasn't lost on me. We made small talk for a few minutes before I headed to my first final of the day. I finished quickly and was relieved that I found it to be pretty easy. I headed to the front of the lecture hall and placed my exam on the desk. After, I went to the library and waited for my next final to start. I looked over my notes before pulling out Noah's letter.

My Jules,

I wrote this because I feared what your reaction would be. I hoped more than anything that I wasn't going to be right. But I know you as well as you know yourself. I want you to know that this was both totally unplanned and unexpected. I was just as surprised as you are. I have spent the last few days trying to find the courage to tell you. I hoped that you wouldn't push me away.

I never wanted to hurt you. All these years that I thought I was protecting you, I now realize how much pain I caused you. (As unintentional as it may have been.) I don't want to be with Carrie and the thought of having a baby with her scares me to death. (I know what you're thinking. I loved her enough at one point to make a baby with her, and now I have to deal with the consequences.)

217

I wish more than anything that it was you in her place. The fact is that I was blind and trying so hard to move on with my life, just to forget you. I didn't see Carrie for what she truly is. I don't expect you to fight this battle with me, but I still wish that you would reconsider. I'm breaking inside. Maybe we can try and work out some kind of custody agreement, anything. Please reconsider this, Jules.

I love you. It's always been you. It will always be you.

You can't leave when I'm still holding on.

Yours,

Noah

I tried to wrap my head around everything. I felt so low. I packed my things into my bag and walked across campus to my last final of the day. I needed to let Noah go. Actually, I needed a hiatus from life.

When I showed up at work later that night, there was a vase of pink peonies, my favorite, with no note. Ellie came bouncing in happily until she saw my face. I told her everything that happened.

"I don't believe it. No fucking way. Jackson hasn't said anything." She paused. "What are you going to do?"

"I called it off between us and that this was too much to move past."

She looked like she wanted to say something more, but she knew better and kept her mouth shut.

"Noah and Jackson are out in the club."

Surprise, surprise.

I headed to Adam's office and knocked.

"I need some time off." I demanded.

He didn't look happy. "I'll see what I do." At least he tried to be understanding.

Next, I waltzed up to Keith and told him I wanted a change of song. I picked three songs instead of two as a farewell. I chose 'Bad Blood' by Taylor Swift, 'Send My Love' by Adele, and 'The Bitch Came Back' by Theory of a Deadman. I stripped down and sashayed out onto the stage, mouthing the lyrics.

I finished out my segment and hurried back to the dressing room. I knew my chances of avoiding Noah were slim, but I was hopeful. I pulled out my notes for my last final tomorrow and started studying. As if my day couldn't get any worse, there was a knock at the door. I turned to see Preacher standing there with an extremely uncomfortable Chase. "Miss Kline, this gentleman said he's a friend of yours."

"It's all right, Preacher; he's fine."

"Ma'am." He tipped his head and walked away, leaving Chase standing there.

"Hey. I got your message and wanted to make sure you were all right. I still can't call your number," he said.

"I'm just fucking dandy." I rolled my eyes.

"I thought of something, and you don't have to go with it, but hear me out." I nodded for him to continue. "I told you I was heading down to stay with my family for a bit. Since you're just about done with finals, I thought maybe you would want to come with me. Just as friends, of course."

"I don't know, Chase. I feel like a ping pong ball." I rubbed my hands over my face, smearing my makeup no doubt. "We broke up, then there was Reid, then Noah. I thought things were finally going right for once. I thought we were going to get a second chance. How wrong was I? I just feel like I can never win and I'm so sick of it!"

220

I was getting emotional again. He stepped in and wrapped his arms around me. I leaned my head onto his shoulder and wrapped my arms around his waist. As much as the idea of getting away sounded peachy right now, I didn't feel right knowing that I would just be using Chase to escape my problems.

I heard someone clear his and I looked over to see Noah standing in the doorway. His neck muscles were bulging and he looked menacing. "Jules," he said tersely.

"Hey." I removed my arms from Chase and took a step away.

"I'm Chase," he said, stepping forward to shake hands with Noah. "You must be Noah." I felt bad for Chase because he was such a good guy, Southern charm and all.

"Chase? As in *Professor Chase Mitchell*?" Noah sneered.

"I used to be a professor. I'm not anymore." Chase turned to look at me. "Think about what I said, Jules. I'll see you later."

"You stay the fuck away from her!" Noah roared angrily. He jerked Chase around by his shirt and pushed him up against the wall.

"STOP!" I yelled. Noah let go, and Chase looked at me. "It's fine," I assured him. He looked hurt, but reluctantly walked out of the dressing room.

221

"Do you mind telling me what the hell just happened?" I yelled at Noah.

He looked slightly embarrassed. "I came back here to talk to you, and I see you with your arms wrapped around some guy. What the hell was that about? You need a rebound already?"

I slapped him as hard as I could, but he crashed his lips to mine. Against my better judgment, I kissed him back pulling the short hairs on the back of his head. His hands roamed up and down my body. I was going to end things the same way they ended ten years ago, but this time on my terms.

Chapter Fourteen: Savior

•◆•◆•◆•◆•◆•◆•◆•◆•◆•◆•◆•◆•◆•◆•

"I love you so much," Noah whispered into my ear.

I didn't have much to take off, so I slid my panties down and undid his belt. I quickly unzipped his jeans and pushed them to his knees. His mouth roamed freely all over my body. I allowed my hands to memorize him for the last time. He lifted me up, so my legs were straddling his waist. He thrust into me, filling me. I rested my head on his shoulder, breathing in the scent that was exclusively Noah. I dug my nails into his back and marked my territory. I allowed myself to feel. With each movement, I felt my heart break a little more. I wanted Noah to have the family he dreamed of, a chance at happiness. I knew I needed to leave in order for that to happen.

He spilled himself into me crying my name. Thankfully, it was quick and passionate because I didn't know how much more resolve I had. He broke our connection and gently placed me on my feet. He brushed the hair out of my face and kissed me lightly. Seeing the love he had for me in his eyes nearly did me in. I told myself not to cry. I needed to be strong for both of us. This was for the best. I dressed quickly and gave him one last fervent kiss.

"Goodbye, Noah," I said, walking toward the back door.

"Goodbye?" He was baffled. By the time reality set in, I was already out the door. "Jules!" he cried, trying to push past Dan.

Seeing Noah drop to his knees and break into tears broke the last remnants of my heart.

I started my car and sped home. I called Chase and told him I would go with him on two conditions. First, he had to hide me for the night so I could take my last exam, and second was that we leave right after. He agreed. It turned out Chase's best friend, Guy, lived in Hoboken, right across the bridge. He was away this week, and Chase said we could stay there since no one would know to look for us at his place. I thanked him.

As soon as I pulled into my driveway, I didn't even bother to shut the car off. I rummaged through my closet and found the biggest suitcase I could. I threw in the first things my hands touched and grabbed my rolled up wad of money so I could buy anything I forgot once we got where we were going. Grabbing my mini backpack full of irreplaceable keepsakes, I looked out the window before making my getaway. I quickly tossed everything into the trunk and sped into the night. Chase texted me the address while

Noah was calling me like a lunatic. I kept hitting ignore but by the sixteenth time, I decided to answer and let him know I was fine.

"Thank God! Jules, what the hell was that?" he choked out.

"What was what?"

"We just… and then you… I've lost you, haven't I?" He sounded so broken I almost caved. Almost.

"You have a family to worry about now, and it's not with me, Noah. You need to get things fixed with Carrie. I'm just helping you with that."

"By running from me?" he asked.

"I'm leaving. I love you and I always will, but it just wasn't meant for us to be together. Fate took care of that for us."

"Don't give up on me just yet," he pleaded. "Where are you going? I'll come with you."

"I don't want you to." The words burned my throat. "I've got to go. Take care of yourself."

"I love you."

I disconnected the call.

225

Not even thirty seconds later, my phone rang again. It was Ellie. I knew I was going to need to explain why I wasn't going to be home for a while. It was going to be hard to be away from her. Especially since we had been inseparable for years. But I also knew I couldn't stay in New York and watch Noah and Carrie raise their baby. I didn't want to be the one to ruin things between Ellie and Jackson, either. She would pick me over him, and they were so good for one another.

"Hey, El," I said, holding back my tears.

"It's not Ellie," a very angry Jackson roared. *Shit!* Well, I was pissed off, too!

"Hi, *Jackson*."

"What the hell is wrong with you, Jules? I thought you were a smart girl."

"Excuse me?" I spat.

"Why are you playing his heart like this? Do you have any idea what kind of hurt he's dealing with right now? Do you?"

"Do you have any idea how hurt I am right now?" I shouted back. "He was my everything, Jackson! Do you think this is what I wanted? No, it's not! I'm not doing this for me! I'm doing this for him! If I'm around, Carrie won't let him be a part of anything to do

226

with the baby. As much as this is hurting him now, that would kill him, and I can't do that to him. I will *not* do that to him!"

"Why can't you guys see what's right in front of your fucking faces? There's a reason that you found each other again."

"Maybe, maybe not," I said. "Either way, he needs to do what's right. He needs you now. Take care of him, Jackson." I clicked off the phone and powered it down.

An hour later, I pulled into a swanky apartment complex in Hoboken. I knocked on the door Chase had told me and he opened it, wearing a pair of plaid pajama bottoms and no shirt. *Damn it!* I knew he was trying to make this difficult for me. Chase was broad shouldered with a chiseled physique. He had an intricate tribal tattoo that sprawled across his entire back.

"You okay?" he asked.

"I will be."

He held his hand out to take the small bag I was carrying and then took my hand with his other one to pull me inside. It was a nice place. The walls were painted a light tan with brown leather furniture. He led me back to the bedroom, which was painted navy blue. A sleigh bed dominated the small space.

227

"There's only one bedroom, so I'll crash on the couch." He turned to head back down the hallway.

"Chase?"

"Yeah?" he asked.

"You can stay in here with me if you want. But *nothing* will happen."

"I don't know." He seemed torn. Chase was one of the good guys.

"Please," I begged.

It was in that moment I realized how broken I was. I needed the comfort of being held, now more than ever. He walked back to the bedroom and lay down on the bed. I grabbed my bag and headed to the adjoining bathroom to shower and change. Once I was in the safety of the shower, I let the tears stream. I hated feeling so weak. I dried my hair and brushed my teeth. I dressed in my sick pajamas and climbed into bed next to Chase. I snuggled close to him and found comfort in the familiarity of his body. He wrapped his arm around my waist.

"Everything's going to be okay, Jules. Sometimes life has a way of testing us and sometimes it's just plain cruel, but things always have a way of working out how they're supposed to.

228

Sometimes the fall kills you, and sometimes when you fall, you fly," he whispered into my hair. I fell asleep wishing for a different ending.

I woke up in an unfamiliar, empty bed. That's when everything came flooding back to me. I put my hand on the pillow where Chase had been sleeping and found a folded up piece of paper.

You're braver than you believe, stronger than you seem, and smarter than you think. ~Winnie the Pooh

He always used to leave things on my pillow when we were together. This particular one resonated with me, especially because I was all of those things. I needed to pull myself together. *I can do this.* I went into the bathroom and checked my face in the mirror. My eyes were slightly puffy from crying, but nothing a little makeup wouldn't cure.

I walked out of the bathroom and went to look for Chase. He was sitting in a recliner, reading the paper and sipping a Starbucks. I eyed it enviously. "I got you one. It's on the counter."

He smiled and I went to retrieve my coffee. "Hey, Jules." I turned to look at him. "We're going to get through this. By the time we're done, you'll come out stronger than ever."

229

I smiled and gave him a kiss on the forehead before getting my coffee. "My exam is at ten. I shouldn't need the full allotted time. I'm hoping to be on the road by eleven-thirty the latest," I said.

"Sure. Sounds good."

I fixed my coffee and turned my phone on quickly to see if there was anything from Ellie. Instead, I was inundated with texts from Noah.

If I never met you, I wouldn't like you. If I didn't like you, I wouldn't love you. If I didn't love you, I wouldn't miss you. But I did, I do, and I always will.

Love me when I least deserve it, because that's when I really need it. I need you so much, Jules. I've been sitting in your driveway all night, and you're not here. I've called every police station and hospital in the city. Please let me know you're okay.

I typed in my text.

I'm fine.

I hit send and shut my phone off. I took one last look at my notes and scrambled so we could get to school on time. It was going to take longer coming from here and supposedly the traffic was a nightmare. We decided we would drive down to North Carolina in my car since Chase already had another one there. I packed up the

230

few things I'd brought and stood in the hallway, waiting for Chase to lock up. When we got to the parking lot, I handed him my keys and sat in the passenger seat. I leaned my head against the window.

"Jules," he said, breaking me out of my reverie. "I know you love Noah, but I think you two got back together way too fast. Honestly, not to sound harsh, but I think it was doomed from the start. He seems like a good guy, but you deserve to find a guy who calls you beautiful instead of hot. Someone who calls you back when you hang up on him, who will stay awake just to watch you sleep. A guy who wants to show off how pretty you look, even in sweats." He eyed my black sweats. "Who thinks you're just as pretty without makeup and reminds you how lucky he is to have you. The guy who says, 'That's her.'"

I knew he was referencing himself, and once again, I was going to have to draw boundaries in sand and blood to keep my heart protected. I had him take a quick detour before we headed to school. Chase pulled into the parking lot at Columbia and I went to check my mailbox for the last time. I left a note for the Academic Records office, letting them know I wouldn't be making the graduation ceremony. I also said that they could mail my diploma to my address in Amityville. I walked into my last final, grabbed an exam off the desk and took a seat in the front row so I could leave as soon as I was done.

Noah

I woke up feeling unsettled. Carrie had called yesterday while Joe and I were at the football game upstate and left a message saying we needed to talk, but she hadn't elaborated. I brushed it off, but then she persistently kept calling, texting, and emailing. She even started harassing Jackson. Finally, I relented and agreed to meet her on Wednesday morning to see what was *so* important. I wanted to tell Jules, but she seemed so fragile after her appointment with Melissa. I knew it had only been a day, but I was starting to get worried. She didn't want to talk about it, so I didn't push.

I trudged out of bed and went for my regular run. I checked my phone and noticed that Carrie had texted me again last night and said it was urgent. I called her before I got in the shower and told her I'd meet her in an hour. I showered and dressed quickly. I kissed Jules on the forehead and headed to Pat's Café. I walked in and saw her sitting in a booth toward the back. She looked slightly disheveled, almost as if she'd been crying. I headed back and took a seat across from her.

"Car, you okay?" I asked.

"No. I don't know." She wasn't her polished, put together self. Even though we weren't together, I still cared about her. I wasn't that much of an asshole.

"What's wrong?" I prodded.

She reached into her purse and pushed something across the table under her hand. I lifted her hand to see what it was. It was a slender, white stick with two pink lines. All the blood left my face. This cannot be happening...

"Is this what I think it is?" I asked, and she started crying again.

"Yes. I'm pregnant, Noah. It's yours."

A million thoughts filtered through my mind. How am I going to tell Jules? What's Jules going to think? This is going to kill Jules. I wish it were Jules. This cannot be happening! I couldn't form a coherent sentence. I just stared at the test in front of me. First, I wanted to punch something; then I realized it could be a blessing in disguise. Since Jules couldn't have children, this would give her an opportunity to be a mom, too. But Carrie was selfish and probably wouldn't like that idea much. At least I had a while to convince her that we could co-parent.

233

We sat in silence for a while as I digested everything. I told her I had to take a little bit to let the news sink in. I hugged her and headed to the office.

I wondered how Robert was going to take it. I texted Jules to tell her to meet me for dinner so we could talk, but before we could meet, I chickened out. I felt like she was still too vulnerable. I sent her a few texts during the week, lying to her and saying I was busy at work. It killed me to do it, and I knew that wouldn't work forever. I needed to grow a pair and tell her the truth.

Finally, I cleared my morning and headed to see her. I knocked on the door and she opened it, looking haggard but still beautiful. She had on an oversized sweatshirt and a pair of plaid shorts. Her hair was in a messy ponytail, and I could tell she had just woken up. I explained to her that I wasn't working all week and instead I was trying to work through some things. I took a deep breath and told her it had to do with Carrie. I just spit it out. "She's pregnant."

At first she looked stunned, then hurt, then angry. *Very angry.* I wanted to hold her and tell her it was going to be okay. She kept me at arm's length, though. I assured her we would get through this together and that it could end up being good for us. I don't think she was even listening to me. Then the switch flipped. She started screaming at me that I had lost my mind. She said she couldn't give

234

this to me, so she was happy for me. She wished me the best and then she started crying; it killed me. I pulled her into my arms, hoping I could show her how much I loved her. I told her I loved her over and over, but she backed away and ran to her room.

I pulled the letter I had written for her that morning out of my pocket and left it by the coffee pot, knowing that she would find it there. I left and headed back to the city and went straight to Jackson's. I wanted his input on the situation. Once I got to his building, I pounded on his door until he opened it.

"What the fuck, dude? Do you know what time it is?" He rubbed his eyes and looked at me. "Oh, man, what happened? Are you okay?"

He grabbed my arm and pulled me inside. He walked straight to the fridge, moving the orange juice aside and opting for a beer; he was going to need it.

"Carrie's pregnant." He spat his beer all over the kitchen.

"What?" he choked.

"Preg-nant," I said, enunciating each syllable.

"How did that happen?" His face was still red from choking.

"Seriously?" I asked, annoyed.

235

"I mean, I know *how*… but I thought she was on the shot thing."

So did I, so did I. "Me, too," I said, running my hands through my hair in utter disbelief. It was as if all the days I had taken to process the news had meant nothing.

"Did you talk to Jules?" he asked. "Is that why you look like someone ran over your puppy?"

"I just came from there. She wants to end things."

"What? She can't do that! How do we even know it's yours?"

"I researched it and, given the timeframe, it would be too early to tell if it were someone else's."

"Fuck!" he said in exasperation. "We'll just have to make Jules see that this could work."

"That's going to be a lot harder than it seems," I told him. "For one, she's stubborn and secondly, she knows that I've always wanted kids. Now that she knows she can't have them, she's hell-bent on making me work things out with Carrie. She wants me to have the family she thinks I want. What she refuses to see is the only reason I wanted a family was because I wanted one with *her*." I started getting emotional.

236

Jackson put his hand on my shoulder. "Man, I'm sorry. This is so screwed up. Should I talk to Ellie?"

"No."

We sat around for most of the day drinking, but we weren't drunk yet. Jackson suggested sending her flowers. I called the florist and arranged a delivery to be sent to her work. After dinner, we took a cab to Double D's. Ellie was sitting at the bar, talking to one of the other girls who worked there; I think her name was Willow. Ellie bounced up as soon as she saw Jackson and ran over, wrapping her legs around his waist and kissing him like a crazy woman. I felt a pang of jealousy. I knew Jules and Ellie were set to go on in a few minutes. I was just hoping to get a chance to talk to Jules between sets. I had to make her see reason.

Ellie went to go finish getting ready. I knew she would most likely tell Jules we were here. Ten minutes later, Jules strolled onto the stage and locked eyes with me. I noticed the song change immediately. I knew the song, because we were both big fans of Three Days Grace. I also knew what she was trying to do, and I was not going to let it happen. The song choice cut me; it talked about being hurt by the ones you loved and trusted the most. Then, the song switched to Theory of a Deadman's 'Bitch Came Back,' and the irony was not lost on me. This was directed at Carrie and I would never be free of her now. She wanted her ring; she got it. It wasn't big enough, and it wasn't the right clarity, yada-yada. No matter what I gave her, it would never be enough, and now I was stuck. *Fuck!*

When Jules walked off the stage, the room burst into applause. I headed to the bar and ordered a shot. I was going to need it. Jackson tried to keep me from going back there until the end of the night, but I was sick of this shit already. We belonged together.

As I drew closer to the dressing room, I overheard a male voice mixed with hers. I saw red. I stormed down the hallway and stopped dead in the doorway when I saw her hugging some tool. She didn't even notice me.

"Jules," I said, trying to control my anger.

She stepped away from the tool, and he took a step towards me. It took all my self-restraint not to pummel him into a speck. He introduced himself as none other than the infamous Chase Mitchell. *Douchebag.*

I moved toward him and told him to stay the fuck away from her. He gave me a look and I lost it. I totally fucking lost it. I grabbed him by his shirt and pushed him hard against the wall, making sure I got a good slam in. His face was about to meet my fist when Jules yelled to cut the shit. Chase left, and she was pissed. Too bad; I was fucking pissed off, too. I started berating her about

238

running off to someone else for a rebound fuck. I wasn't surprised when she slapped me. I deserved it.

I lowered my head enough so I could capture her lips and I kissed her with everything I had in me. I professed my love over and over like a lovesick fool. She moved my pants to my knees and I happily obliged. When I finally slid into her, I was in my happy place, lost in Jules. I could have happily stayed like that forever. I pushed her up against the door and thrust into her over and over. She tightened, and I let myself go at the same time she did. I loved this girl so fucking much it hurt. I watched her get dressed, but I was confused; it was only the beginning of the night. I was hoping that she would offer to go back to my place so I could spend the night reassuring her that everything was going to be okay. Instead, she leaned in and kissed me.

"Goodbye, Noah." She stalked out the back door.

I wanted to chase after her, but there was no way to get past the goon guarding the door. I tried calling her, but she wouldn't answer. I called right back. Finally, she picked up and we had a bit of a fight. She told me I needed to fix things with Carrie and that she was my family now. Then she told me that she was leaving. *Leaving...*

239

I told her I loved her before she hung up on me. I crumbled to the ground, clutching my phone, and I put my head between my legs. I cried like I'd never cried in my life. For some reason, this was even worse than it was the last time. Probably because it involved an innocent life and things were entirely out of our control, once again.

Eventually, I headed home to wallow in self-pity. It literally hurt to breathe. I couldn't allow myself to admit that it was over. She still needed me to hold her. She was testing me. She had to be.

I texted her a couple times and didn't get a response. I started to panic. I ran to the parking garage and hopped in my Jeep. The only thing that I could think of was that she was so upset when she left that she had been in an accident, or something awful had happened. I sped like a madman to her house, but her car wasn't there. She should have been home for over an hour. She wouldn't have left already since there was nowhere for her to go.

I sat there like a statue. Her phone was off, and every possible scenario ran through my head. Ellie hadn't heard from her, either. I started calling hospitals, then police stations. I was in a full-blown panic. I stared at her door for hours, waiting for her to come home. She never did; instead, I got a text in the morning, saying *I'm fine.* I tried calling her back, but she had already turned her phone off. I knew I should probably go to work today since I hadn't gone the day before, but I couldn't force myself to move.

240

My phone rang. I answered it on the first ring. "Jules," I cried.

"No!" Carrie replied harshly. "Trouble in paradise?"

"No, everything's fine," I lied.

"Sure it is," she spat sarcastically. "I just wanted to see what you were doing today. I wanted to go look at some furniture for the nursery."

"Don't people usually wait until they're a little further along before they do that?" I asked.

"I want to see what they have. I'll probably end up ordering something custom. I just want to see what options are available." *What had I gotten myself into?*

"I'm not really feeling well today. Maybe another time."

"Fine. But you're not avoiding me forever, Noah Sinclair." She hung up.

I backed out of Jules' driveway and headed back to my condo. I mustered the nerve to call Robert and tell him I wasn't going to make it in, again. "I hope you're going to do what's right, son," he said before hanging up.

241

This just keeps getting better and better. I crawled into bed and fell apart. I clenched my pillow and felt something. There was a piece of paper under my pillow.

Never forget me, because if I thought you would, I'd never leave.

X, J

She had come here!

A week went by, then two and three. It had been a month since I'd heard from Jules. Ellie was tight lipped. She just said that Jules had moved on, and that she was happy. She wanted me to do the same, but I couldn't. I didn't want to. I tried to use the lost phone app to find out where she was, but her phone was never on. It didn't stop me from trying, though. Every single day.

Carrie had become more persistent about doing things together to strengthen our relationship before the baby came. I reluctantly gave her one night a week. Part of me felt horrible. I should be treating her better because she was going to be the mother of my child, but I just wasn't there yet. Instead, I resented her for what had happened with Jules. I decided I needed to go home. I needed to clear my head.

I booked a flight that left the next day and returned Sunday afternoon. I needed my mom. I called and let them know I was coming home. She knew I was struggling with Jules being gone again, but I had yet to tell her about the baby. I wasn't sure how she was going to react, and it needed to be a face-to-face conversation.

I packed my suitcase and forced myself to go to sleep. Every time I closed my eyes, all I saw was Jules. The way I felt about her just wouldn't go away. I clutched to that piece of paper to myself like it was my lifeline. She haunted my dreams. She was 'the one.'

I just wanted to run away. I spent the night tossing and turning. In the morning, I filled a mug with coffee and headed down to the lobby to meet with Segundo. We headed to JFK so I could catch my flight. Jackson called me on the way. "Hey, man." He sounded glum about something.

"Morning, Jax." I sounded like a zombie.

"I was wondering if you wanted to meet up for lunch or something?" he asked. It made me suspicious. I had known him long enough to know when he was trying to avoid something.

"Can't. I'm on my way to the airport. I decided to head home for the weekend."

243

"Why didn't you mention it? I would have come with you. I miss June-bug." He was referring to my mom.

"That's exactly why I didn't mention it," I said. "I need to go alone. I need time to think about things. I don't know what to do about Jules, or Carrie, or anything right now."

"I'm pretty sure Jules is gone for good, bro."

"What makes you say that?" I asked. Bingo. That was probably what he wanted to talk to me about. Ellie must have found something out. I dreaded what was about to come out next…

"This morning, Ellie was making breakfast…"

"And?"

"Well… she got a message from Jules. Except it wasn't a text. It was a picture."

"Okay…" I waited for him to continue.

"She was kissing Chase and holding her hand in front of the camera. It looked like she was sporting an engagement ring or something."

"It's probably the ring I gave her," I quickly argued.

244

"No. It was a different one. I'm positive. Anyway, I forwarded the picture to my phone. I can send it to you if you want?" he asked.

"Yeah, send it over." My heart beat out of my chest as each second ticked by. Normally, I would find the ride to the airport relaxing, but today it was anything but.

"Call me if you need to talk," he told me.

"Thanks, Jax."

I disconnected the call and waited for the message. As soon as it arrived, I opened it. Sure enough, it was a picture of Jules and Chase. They were kissing on a blanket. Her hand was in the foreground and she was showcasing a diamond engagement ring.

My heart shattered. I felt like I was going to throw up. How could she do this to me? I was trying my best to hold it together, but I was devastated. That should be my ring on her finger.

After I got to the airport, I made it through security with plenty of time to spare. I stopped for a drink at one of the restaurants. I didn't give a shit that it was only ten in the morning. I sat there until it was time to board. I couldn't stop myself from looking at every blonde who passed by, hoping to see her face.

After a short and uneventful flight, I grabbed my carry-on and headed to the rental car pick-up. Then, I started towards home. The picture of Jules and Chase was still burned into my mind. It was all I could think about. An hour later, when I pulled into the driveway, my mom came out and greeted me. She pulled me into a giant hug and pulled me down so she could kiss my forehead. Being the momma's boy I was, I broke down and started crying.

"Come on, sweetheart," she said. "Let's go inside, and you can tell me all about what's going on." My mom, June, didn't look at day over forty-five. She was petite and slender with dark brown hair and blue eyes. She was the kindest woman I knew.

I followed her inside and left my bag in the foyer. She led me into the kitchen. "I made you a pecan pie." She cut a slice and put it on a plate, sliding it in front of me and handing me a fork. I took a bite. It was delicious, as always.

"Now tell me what's going on," she said.

I started filling her in. I was dreading dropping the baby bomb. She had the look like she was going to offer me some advice.

"Honey, you can shed tears that she is gone, or you can smile because you had the time you did with her. You can close your eyes and pray that she'll come back, or you can open your eyes and see that she left. Your heart is empty because you can't see her, but let it

246

be full because of the love you shared. Cherish the memories of the times you spent together and let it live on, but she's not yours anymore. Do you think this is what Jules would want?" she asked. It sounded like she was talking about someone's death. I guess in a way that's almost how I felt about the whole thing.

"There's more to the story than that," I said. "Remember when I told you that Jules met with Melissa, and she said conception didn't look good for us?" I felt bad because my mom didn't know the reason that Jules couldn't have kids. I didn't want her to have to carry that around. Not now.

"Of course I remember, but that's no reason for her to run away," she said solemnly.

"Well, I found something out a few days after that. I've been trying to work through it. It's the reason Jules took off and why I needed to come home to clear my head." She nodded for me to continue and placed her small hand in mine. "Carrie told me she's pregnant. It's mine," I said sadly.

I should be ecstatic, but my heart is fighting me every step of the way. Carrie isn't the one I want to share this with.

"Oh dear." Her mouth dropped open.

247

"Tell me about it. I told Jules. I hoped we would be able to do this together. I wanted to do this together. She told me I needed to go back to Carrie and work things out. Then she left. This isn't how it was supposed to end, Mom." I fought back tears again. "I haven't been able to get in touch with Jules at all. I don't know where she is, but I know she's with her ex, Chase. Then, right before I got to the airport this morning, Jackson told me he saw a picture on Ellie's phone." I pulled my phone out and showed her the photo.

"Oh, honey, you're going to experience the best gift life has to offer. You're going to be a father, an amazing one at that. Maybe Jules was right by doing what she did. I know you don't see it that way now, but one day you will. She knew you wouldn't have the chance to experience it fully if she was in the picture. Think of it as a gift."

A gift, my ass. I wanted the baby and Jules.

"Mom, it's too hard. I've loved Jules for as long as I can remember. I went all those years thinking I would never see her again. I got her back only to have her leave again. This time, she left on her own terms. I really thought I was ready to move on when I met Carrie, and I tried; I genuinely did. After being with Jules again, though, I know that she's the one. I want to be with Jules!"

"Honey, it looks like she made her choice," my mother said. "I'm sorry, but it wasn't you. You need to do the right thing here, for the baby's sake." I could always trust her to tell me like it is. I respected her for that.

"I don't know if I can," I admitted.

"You can and you will. You're a grown man now, Noah. I raised you better than that." I nodded in understanding. "Now, when you go back to New York, I want you to beg, plead, grovel, whatever you need to do to get back in good graces with the mother of my grandbaby. You understand?"

"Yes, ma'am."

"Good." She kissed my cheek and flitted around the kitchen. "I'm making chicken and dumplings for you. Go take your things to your room and get ready to come eat."

I spent the majority of my trip in my room staring at Jules' old window. I was still feeling torn, but I knew what I had to do. It was going to kill me.

Carrie ♡

This is not going as planned. What's taking him so long to come around? The bitch is out of the way, and this bitch is ready to get her man. Looks like I got them both by the Achilles heel.

"Everything's going as planned," the voice said.

"Excellent. Let's just hope he takes the bait." I trailed my fingertips over my abdomen and disconnected from the call.

My phone rang again. It was Noah. "Is everything alright?" I asked sweetly.

"Fine, I just wanted to let you know I'm in Georgia for a couple days. I'd like to see you when I get back. I was hoping to schedule an appointment with Melissa this week for an ultrasound."

I hated that bitch, too. "I already have a doctor, and it's too early to see anything yet anyway," I told him.

"Okay. I'll see you in a few days then."

"Be safe."

"Bye, Carrie." He sounded miserable, but I wasn't going to let that knock me off my pedestal. I finally had Noah Sinclair exactly where I wanted him.

Chapter Fifteen:
Over and Over

•◦•◦•◦•◦•◦•◦•◦•◦•◦•◦•◦•◦•◦•

Jules ♡

"We have to make this look as convincing as possible," I told Chase.

My heart was breaking more with each step. I had been talking to Ellie at least a couple times a week since our arrival here. She told me that Noah had been doing nothing except moping around since I'd left. He was even ignoring Jackson. I needed him to do the right thing. Chase and I formulated a plan to push him in the right direction. We had been hiding out at his grandfather's cabin in rural North Carolina since we'd left New York. The circumstances weren't the greatest, but we were making the best of it.

Chase reminded me of all the reasons I had loved him in the first place. He was so loyal and protective. I was thankful for

253

everything he'd helped me through over the past month. Although we slept in the same bed every night, we maintained a strict "friendship only" relationship. I couldn't deny that I enjoyed the comfort and security it brought, but I knew I was asking him to cross the line today. I worried it would ignite old feelings. However, I wasn't ready to put Noah behind me yet. I was still grieving him; I would probably grieve him for the rest of my life.

Although Noah and I had only been back together for a short time, it was as if no time had passed between us at all. We were made for each other. At the same time, I loved him enough to want what was best for him, even if it was killing me.

Chase led me down to the dock, where he'd set up our photo-op. I took a deep breath and sat on the blanket. I had my Trac-phone in my right hand and his grandmother's ring on my left. We leaned back and kissed as I hit the camera button, making sure that the ring was in the picture. I looked at the picture. It looked convincing. I sat up and quickly pressed send.

Ellie had been sure to place her phone where Jackson would see it. Jackson, being the drama king he was, would make sure Noah saw it. I just hoped it would be the ammunition that he needed to go back to Carrie. *I don't think he knows how much he wants this.* I knew this marked the end of the Noah and Jules saga. At this point my heart was already broken, though, and I just wanted to make sure

254

one of us made it out with a happily ever after. As soon as it was delivered, I slid the ring off my finger and handed it back to Chase.

"It looked good there. Maybe someday you'll let me put it there for real." He smiled. He was trying to make it sound like a joke, but I wasn't buying it.

I slid Noah's promise ring back onto my finger and headed back to the cabin. I knew I was about to have a moment and I just wanted to be alone. As soon as I walked into the bedroom, I closed the door behind me. I climbed into bed and broke into tears. I was grateful for what Chase had done and kept doing for me, but I was starting to feel crowded. He kept pushing for *more.* It wasn't fair to keep stringing him along, either. I spent the afternoon crying on and off. Chase came in a little while later and offered me his shoulder. I guiltily accepted.

"What can I do to make you love me like that, Jules? I would do anything. I love you so much. I wish you could see that," he pleaded.

"You know you can't help who you love. It just happens. I do love you. Just not like that, not anymore. I'm sorry. You're an incredible man, Chase Mitchell, but I'm not sure I'll ever find another Noah."

I slid out from next to him and put my sneakers on. I needed to take a walk around the lake so I could clear my head. I felt bad that Chase's helping me was hurting him. I needed to find another alternative.

Time was moving in slow motion, but I'd make it another two more weeks. Ellie texted me that Noah was trying to spend more time with Carrie. I was both pleased and devastated. Chase continued his efforts to win me over. They were starting to wear me down, though, and I knew I needed to leave. When I told him I was thinking about leaving, he went into an absolute panic. He said there was nothing left for me at home, and all of my suffering would be in vain if I went back now. He was right, and I couldn't think of where else I could possibly go.

I went to lie down in the bedroom. I started asking myself, *why me? Why do I always get the shit hand?* I knew I needed to get away; being with Chase was just making it more difficult.

I turned on my real phone for the first time in over a month and a half and scrolled to a number I hadn't used in three years. My dad. My message indicator continually blinked throughout our brief conversation. They were all from Noah. There was one a day for the first month, and some sporadic ones over the last few weeks. They ranged from *I love you* and *I miss you*, to desperate pleas for me to come home and work things out.

"The ticket will be at the kiosk," my dad said. "I'll have Harry come collect you from the airport. I'm glad you called, Juju."

I hung up and headed out to tell Chase I was leaving. "We need to talk," I said. He was watching a documentary and he looked content. I hated myself even more.

"What's up?" He put his hand out and pulled me down, so I was sitting in his lap. I rubbed my hand on his cheek.

"I'm leaving." I hugged him. "I need to go. It's time. Thank you for everything."

"You can't leave. Please don't leave me," he pleaded. "I love you, Jules. You're my Noah." That last part tugged at my heart because that's the kind of love that doesn't just go away. I knew that pain firsthand. A single tear fell from his cheek.

"I'm sorry, Chase." I stood up and went to pack my things.

My phone chimed, and I realized I had forgotten to turn it back off. Of course it was from Noah.

He sent me the YouTube video for Three Doors Down's 'Without You'.

I can't think of anything more fitting even if I tried. I know where you are now. I'm not going to chase you. I'll see you in my dreams tonight and I'll love you forever. Noah.

Jackson and I were sitting in his kitchen; Ellie had just arrived. The two of them were so in love. It was sickening to watch. They were going to end up together, whether they wanted to admit it or not. Jackson had grudgingly allowed Carrie to come over for a little while, but she quickly ducked out as soon as Ellie showed up. I knew she wasn't Ellie's number one fan, and Ellie was most certainly not hers, but I still couldn't understand why Carrie refused to be in the same room as her. At least Ellie made an effort to be cordial towards her.

"Noah, how many weeks is Carrie now?" Ellie asked.

"Eighteen, almost nineteen. Why?" I could sense that this wasn't an out of the blue question.

"Because that's how far along Jules was when she lost the baby. She had a pretty good bump by then. Carrie doesn't have one at all."

"Some people carry differently than others," I said quickly, almost defensive.

"Chill, bro, it was just a statement," Jackson snapped.

I knew I'd been being a super asshole ever since my phone finder app had alerted me to Jules' whereabouts last week. I had not been happy to find out that she was staying with Chase. I guess I'd still been in denial. She'd left with him, and they were supposedly engaged now, but I wanted to drive down there and bring her home. Jackson begrudgingly reminded me of my place now, and it wasn't with Jules.

Ever since my trip back home, I'd actually been trying to work things out with Carrie. I even went as far as recently re-proposing to her, so we could get married before the baby's arrival. She, of course, was over the moon, but she'd made a snarky remark about the ring. It was the same ring I had given her the last time. I brushed it off. I was willing to do anything at this point for my, *our* baby. I'd suffer the rest of my life with her if it meant that I could be with my son or daughter.

"Sorry," I apologized.

"I just think the whole thing is weird. She refuses to see Melissa, one of the best OB/GYNs in the city and every time she has an 'appointment'" Ellie air quoted, "she miraculously forgets to tell you. We have yet to see an ultrasound picture, too. Jules had one at twelve weeks, Noah."

Her name was like a Taser to my system every time. I've never heard Ellie talk about the baby in detail before. I knew she'd been around during the whole pregnancy, but she had never talked about it until now.

"What do you want me to tell you?" I snapped again.

"Have you been sleeping together?" Ellie snapped back.

"No. I can't," I stammered. I didn't even see Carrie like that anymore. How was I supposed to marry someone I didn't even want to kiss?

"So you haven't seen her naked? I'm just saying this doesn't make much sense. I'm just trying to protect you, so stop being an asshole to me." She turned and went to the living room. She pulled out her phone and started texting. I wondered if she was texting Jules. I instantly got jealous.

"She has a point, man," Jackson said. "I mean, she's rushing to get you back to the altar, and some things are obviously off, especially since Ellie brought that stuff up. Just be careful."

"I'll see you guys later," I said and headed out.

I thought about how I had just re-proposed last week, and she had already mailed the wedding invitations out. Our wedding was supposed to take place in two weeks. *Two weeks!* She said she didn't want to be too big to fit in her dress, which made sense to me. However, the more I thought about it, she wasn't big at all.

I pushed that thought aside and headed home. I ordered a pizza and decided to call Melissa. She would know the answers. We had been talking a lot because of my first time dad questions.

"Hello, Noah," she answered on the third ring.

"Hey, Melissa. Do you have a minute?" I asked.

"Sure, give me a minute to close the door." She paused. "All right, shoot."

"I was with Jackson and Ellie before, and they brought up a couple things that I wanted to talk to you about."

"I'm all ears," she said.

261

"Ellie said that when Jules was pregnant, she'd had an ultrasound at twelve weeks. Is that normal?" I asked.

"Yes. Usually we do one around then to check the baby's development. In most cases, we usually do one even earlier to pinpoint an accurate due date. They're usually done at twelve weeks, twenty weeks, and then at least another two are done before delivery to track fetal development and to make sure there aren't any issues. Carrie has had one, right?" she asked.

"Not that I know of. I haven't seen any ultrasound pictures, and she hasn't mentioned one."

"Well, she should have her twenty week checkup in a little over two weeks. That's when you can find out the gender, but she should have had one already."

I took a deep breath and processed the information. My hand was starting to tremble. Two weeks... "She's also not really showing at all."

"That could be something to worry about, but remember, all women carry differently. Some don't start to show until they're at five or six months, especially with their first. Do you know who her attending is? I've asked her a couple times, but she outright ignores me."

"I think she goes to Luanne Garba," I said. "I'm not sure."

"Listen, I'll see what I can find out for you. Luanne is affiliated with the same hospital as me. Next time, I'm there for a delivery, I'll see if I can pull Carrie's records. But Noah, this stays between us."

"I'd really appreciate that, Melissa. Thank you."

"Anytime. I'll be in touch." She disconnected the call.

I walked to my end table and picked up Jules' note, holding it between my fingers. I'd never forget her.

As I was eating my dinner, a text popped up. My heart went into overdrive when I saw the sender. It was from Jules.

I miss you, too. Just so you know, there's a space that only you can fill. Just so you know, I loved you then, and I guess I always will. We both need to move on now. Be happy, Noah.

My heart jumped into my throat.

I don't know how to be happy without you. I've tried. It's just so fucking hard! You ruined me. I love YOU! I replied.

Nobody said it would be easy, but you'll figure it out. Take care.

Two Weeks Later...

Melissa called me two days before the wedding was supposed to take place and turned my world upside down. Again. She apologized for not getting back to me sooner and asked me to meet her for lunch. I told her I could meet her in forty minutes. When I saw her at the restaurant, she looked like a celebrity hiding from the paparazzi. She slid over so I could slip into the booth next to her and flagged the waiter. When she ordered me a double Jack, I knew it wasn't good news.

"Noah," She placed her tiny hand on top of mine. "I looked up Carrie's records yesterday and there is nothing, other than a normal checkup three months ago. They even ran blood and urine screens. Even if she were only a couple of weeks pregnant, the blood work would have picked it up. She's not pregnant, Noah."

I felt betrayed like I'd been the asshole or the brunt of some sick joke. I was going to pass out... or throw up... or throw something. The waiter placed the shot on the table. Melissa pushed it in front of me and I downed it quickly. I needed to confront Carrie,

264

but my mind instantly went to Jules. She was the only one who could probably save me from this darkness I was falling into.

I thanked Melissa and headed out on a mission. I made a couple phone calls and decided that revenge is a dish best served cold. She wanted to make a joke out of me? I'd do her one better.

Jules

I had been in England for a little over two weeks. I was enjoying getting to know my younger brother, Harry. I pretty much avoided my dad. Even though he'd allowed me to come here, it turns out zebras don't change their stripes. We tried talking a few times, but things were just too far gone. There was too much hurt for us to have a real relationship.

Harry, on the other hand, was a great kid. He helped me keep my mind off of things back home. It was weird at first because he was eighteen and we'd never met before, but we bonded quickly. His mom, Meredith, seemed nice enough. I hadn't spent much time trying to get to know her, either. I had a small loft to myself with a private entrance. No one other than my dad knew where I took off to. Not even Ellie.

"So, tell me about the States," Harry said.

"What do you want to know?" I laughed.

"What are your mates like? What do you do for fun? Stuff like that." He had the most adorable British accent.

"Well, my best friend back home is Ellie. She's awesome. We live together in a little house outside New York City, and we worked together. She's really funny. We met at boarding school when I was sixteen. We have been best friends ever since."

"What did you do for work?" he asked. *How was I supposed to answer that?*

"Um, I, um… I danced," I stuttered.

"Like ballet?"

"Something like that." I smiled.

"What about your other friends? Dad said something about some bloke, and that's the reason you were coming here."

"That would be Noah. He was my best friend growing up. My mom is not like yours. She's vindictive and likes things to go her way. When I was sixteen, she forced me to move with her to New York. Noah and I were separated, but we found each other again not too long ago. We had a whirlwind romance. Then some things happened, and here I am." I tried to muster some enthusiasm.

"He didn't hurt you, did he? I'd kill him if he did." It was so adorable how he stuck up for me. Although he could probably defend me if necessary. He was a big kid. He was into boxing and wrestling. He was also on a rugby team. I had even gone to a couple of his matches since my arrival.

"No. He didn't hurt me, not like you're thinking. Just some grown up stuff that neither of us had any control of." I patted his shoulder.

I walked over to the end table and pulled out a picture of Noah and me, handing it to him.

"You both look really happy here," he said. "Whatever happened, maybe you could get past it. You only get one life, no dress rehearsal. You should make the best out of every day because there is no guarantee that you are going to wake up tomorrow."

"You're awfully wise for being so young, Harry. We've made our peace, and we're moving on. I'll get there one day. I'm just not ready yet."

267

I held back my tears as he handed me the photo. I ran my thumb over Noah's beautiful face before placing the picture back in the drawer. Harry and I talked for a couple more hours and watched a movie before turning in for the night. At three in the morning, my phone started ringing off the hook. I reached over to see who it was. It was Chase. I declined the call, but it kept ringing. Again and again. I knew there had to be some reason for him calling me this early in the morning.

"What?" I barked.

"Jules, there's a problem. I need to talk to you. You're going to hate me." He was speaking a mile a minute. When he was finished, my blood was boiling.

"You fucking did *what*?" I screamed. "Please tell me you're kidding, Chase!"

"I'm so, so sorry."

I hung up before he could say anything else. I called the airline and booked the first flight I could get. I went to say goodbye to Harry and told him that he better come visit me soon. I promised I would be back. I didn't want to wake my dad, so I left him a note and went outside to wait for the taxi.

Noah

I didn't even look at the speedometer; I knew I was going well above the posted speed limit following the GPS directions. Randall had flown me to the nearest heliport in his private helicopter. He even had a rental waiting for me when we landed. When I called him earlier, I started to tell him what happened. I didn't even get out more than two sentences before he told me to meet him. He said he would take me himself. Randall was a man with connections galore, and this was one of the times that I was grateful for each and every one of them.

When I pulled up to the little cabin in a secluded part of North Carolina, I saw a familiar car. It was Jules' Infiniti. I barreled into the driveway and started pounding down the door like a madman. Jules didn't answer; Chase did. I punched him, because deep down, I somehow knew he had something to do with this.

"Where is she?" I bellowed. I started walking around and opening every door.

"She's not here."

"What the fuck do you mean she's not here? Where is she?" I lifted him by his shirt and jacked him up against the wall.

"I don't know. She left about two weeks ago. She didn't tell me where she was going. I swear."

"You knew, didn't you? You sick and twisted little fuck! You were part of the plan all along, weren't you?" I yelled.

"It wasn't supposed to end like this. You were supposed to marry Carrie, and I was going to get back together with Jules. No one was supposed to get hurt."

I couldn't help myself. I punched him again. I was seething. "You selfish prick!" I screamed in his face. "Did you not think of how Jules felt?"

"I didn't. I thought I could get her to change her mind. I thought if she had enough time she would heal. She would get over you, especially since she wanted you to work things out so badly with Carrie that she set up a fake engagement. I figured if she knew you guys were done, she would finally give me a second chance."

"Did you know that Carrie wasn't pregnant?" I asked.

"What? No. She is. I saw the test and everything." The lawyer in me knew he was telling me the truth.

"She's not. She never was. It was all a hoax."

I let go of him, and he slid to the ground, dropping his head into his hands.

"Listen, I slashed her tires but Carrie was the mastermind. She was also the one who had come up with the school scandal in hopes of ruining Jules' chances at getting her degree." He cringed. "I couldn't let that happen. That's why I resigned.

I was ready to break his face, but I decided I needed his help.

"You fucked up, and now you're going to help me fix it," I said.

"How?" He looked up incredulously.

I delved into the plan, and he listened patiently. I crossed my fingers and hoped for the best.

I woke up relaxed and refreshed. Today, I would be Mrs. Carrie Sinclair and Noah would be mine. Finally. Of course, I was going to have to fake a terrible miscarriage, but I would make sure that it only brought us closer. I had stopped my shot months ago, so I shouldn't have any trouble getting the deal done for real this time.

I headed to go get my morning coffee. I walked in and saw that stupid bitch, Melissa, and who was with her, other than my second least favorite person, Ellie. I hated that whore almost as much as I hated *Jules.*

"Getting ready for the big day?" they asked. I was not happy that they were on the guest list, but Noah had insisted.

"Yep. Only a couple more hours." I rubbed it in a little more than necessary. There was no way they were knocking me down. *Not today, bitches!*

I headed over to the hotel where we were getting married and checked into the penthouse suite. I waited for my bridesmaids to show up and I was sipping on a vodka tonic when the first of my guests arrived. All my friends knew the baby was a lie, but they were just as vindictive as I was and didn't care.

There was a knock, and when I opened the door, there was a room service cart filled with champagne and my favorite mini desserts. They must be from Noah. I popped an éclair in my mouth and finished my drink. It's going to be a fabulous day!

Jules

By the time I touched town at Newark International Airport, I was both physically and emotionally exhausted. When Chase called and told me what he'd done, I was beyond appalled. The amount of betrayal I felt made me sick to my stomach because I trusted him. I was also outright pissed at Carrie, that conniving bitch. She knew damn well Chase would go along with her plan. She preyed on his vulnerability and used it to push Noah and me apart.

I felt absolutely disgusting from all the travel. I grabbed my luggage off the turnstile; Melissa and Ellie were waiting for me by the baggage claim. Ellie was holding a sign that read, "The real Mrs. Sinclair," which made me smile. She tossed the sign on the ground and practically knocked me on my ass as she ran to embrace me. I gave Melissa a hug, too.

"Thanks so much for coming to collect me."

"I missed you *so* much!" Ellie cooed wrapping her arms around me again.

"I missed you, too." I patted her head.

273

"Come on, let's go! We have a plan to put into action," Ellie said with an evil laugh.

We got into Melissa's Range Rover and headed towards NYC. Melissa explained to me her findings on Carrie. I was shocked all over again hearing it from her. She had been the one to tell Noah. She said we would have never known, though, if it weren't for Ellie's persistence.

Ellie climbed into the back and rustled through my suitcase, looking for something suitable for me to wear. She tossed a navy colored wrap dress at me and found a thick, brown belt that went well with it. She untangled my hair and applied some makeup, making me look presentable. I didn't have much in terms of shoes, so Melissa took off her brand new Tory Birch flats and handed them to me. They happened to be the same color as the belt. She winked and said to think of them as a welcome home present.

I was lucky to have such great people in my life. It made me feel even more terrible for shutting everyone out when things went bad. It's hard when you run in the same circle. You don't want to make people choose. That would have been especially hard with Ellie dating Jackson and Melissa being married to Joe. I had honestly wanted Noah to try and forget me. I had wanted him to do the right thing, even though it killed me. Now that I knew the truth, I was going to let that spoiled bitch have what was coming to her. She was going to be sorry she'd ever heard the name Julia Kline.

Ellie glanced at her phone and told me that phase one had been put into place.

"What is phase one?" I asked curiously.

"You know that kid Brian, who comes into the club sometimes?" I nodded. He was a friend of Brad's. "Well… he happens to work at the hotel where they're supposed to be getting married." I nodded again. "I had a nice delivery of laxative-laced treats sent to her room. Noah said she's a sucker for éclairs, so I made sure there were *plenty* of them. In about an hour she's going to be shitting her brains out."

I looked at the clock and realized that they only had about an hour before the ceremony was going to start. I laughed. I wanted to feel bad. I really did, but after everything she had put me through, it didn't even seem close to vengeance.

Forty minutes later, we were sneaking in through the back door of the hotel. A very chipper Jackson greeted us. He pulled Ellie to him and kissed her passionately, before engulfing me in a hug. I was glad to see the two of them were still going strong. They made a great couple.

275

"I'm so glad you're here, Jules," he whispered into my ear. "It's been hell without you and no one can stand what wench."

"Where's Noah?"

"He'll be here soon. Don't worry." Jackson said.

I stood next to Melissa and thanked her again. I laughed as I looked at her immaculate outfit with my dingy running sneakers. She just shrugged and smiled. Ellie told Jackson what she had done as phase one. He was practically on the ground, he was laughing so hard.

"I love you, woman. I really do."

I was anxious to see Noah. I had missed him like crazy. Jackson was leading us in a covert mission through the hotel lobby when a familiar set of red claws dug into my arm, halting me in my tracks. I turned and gasped.

"Well, well, if it isn't the whore, trying to get in the way of the happy couple." Abigail sneered.

Jackson looked at Ellie with wide eyes. My palm started to twitch. I controlled it since I didn't want to start a scene. We didn't need any unwanted attention. "What are you doing here?" I spat.

"Oh, I was invited, sweetheart. Unlike you." She looked the same, a little older, but the same. She still has the same fucking nails, too!

"Who invited you, Abigail?" Ellie asked, getting in her face.

"I don't go by Abigail anymore. I go by Libby now." Something flashed in Jackson's face. "That's right. I'm Libby Collins, Carrie's aunt." *Oh my God!*

"You were behind this the whole time, weren't you?" I asked.

"Oh, darling, I love nothing more than seeing you as miserable as you've made me," she said.

"That's why we couldn't find any recent information on you," Jackson mumbled.

"I didn't know that Noah was the same Noah at first. However, as soon as I did, I made sure that we never had the pleasure of meeting. I did everything I could to make sure he would never know that I was part of the happy family. I even made a point to avoid any work function where he might be. When Carrie came to Robert crying, saying that Noah had called off the engagement, she mentioned your name. I knew that you'd gotten your filthy claws back into him. You don't deserve him, You never have. I made sure

277

that Carrie had the information she needed to win him back." She was referring to my baby, the same baby that she'd made me lose. "We found out how bad the Mitchell boy had it for you and worked him into our little plan as well. I knew you would take off. You've got your father's disgusting conscience."

I was shaking and having a hard time staying upright when a familiar scent hit me. I'd know it anywhere. I sucked in a deep breath. "Abigail, what are you doing here?" Noah demanded.

"Is that any way to speak to your future mother-in-law?"

He looked confused as he wrapped his arms around me. I felt safe like that. I turned my head slightly so I could look at his profile. He looked haggard but still breathtaking. She couldn't hurt me as long as he was holding me. He gave me the strength I needed to stand up to her for the first time in my life. She stood there with a smirk on her face as we filled in the gaps for him.

"Abigail, you need a high five in the face, with a chair," Ellie said.

I looked her straight in the eye and said my piece. "You are so self-absorbed! You have *never* cared about anyone except for yourself, ever. You have never been a mother to me. For a long time, it made me sad, but you know what? I'm actually grateful because if you hadn't made me into that shy, broken little girl that needed

278

someone like I needed Noah we probably wouldn't have known that we were soul mates. And guess what? I'm much stronger now. I'm standing here with this group of incredible friends and the guy whom I love more than my own life and all of that is because you showed me everything that love isn't."

"You're nothing but a bitch," she said.

"If I were really a bitch, I'd make your life a living hell. Instead, I'll just stand by and watch you do that yourself. You seem to do a pretty good job at it."

Robert was standing within earshot. I knew he'd overheard most of what was going on. He approached slowly and Abigail started the dramatics. He looked slightly perplexed, so Noah and Ellie filled him in on the rest. When they finished, Robert looked green. Jackson brought over a chair for him so he could sit.

The wedding was supposed to start in ten minutes, and Carrie was going to feel a bit of what Noah and I had been feeling for the last two months. Alone. Ellie was hoping she would shit herself in front of everyone. Jackson seemed to have everything under control. Noah pulled me into the stairwell and pushed me against the wall, claiming my mouth with his. I forgot everything and lost myself in his kiss. I wrapped my arms around his neck and pulled him as close as I could. We kissed until we were out of breath. He pulled away and looked me in the eyes.

"I missed you so much." He had tears streaming down his cheeks. He put his hands on the side of my face as if he was trying to reassure himself that I was really there. I leaned in and kissed him again for reassurance.

"I never left you," I said, putting my hand on his heart. "I've always been here." My own tears started flowing.

Jackson tapped on the door, interrupting. "Sorry to break up the reunion, but it's show time."

Noah tugged on my hand as we moved swiftly through the corridor to where Melissa and Ellie were standing. Apparently, Robert was furious and he had hotel security holding Abigail until the ceremony was done. He had agreed to go along with the plan because he believed in tough love. More than that, he believed in true love and he wished Noah and me nothing but the best.

We had a perfect vantage point to see everything but we were where we couldn't be spotted. We watched as Carrie came through the lobby with her posse. They went down the aisle, one by one. I watched as Chase stood with his back to the crowd, filling in for Noah. They did a great job. Even I couldn't tell the difference from

280

the back. Carrie walked arm-in-arm with Robert down the aisle. I leaned my head on Noah's shoulder and he turned and smiled at me.

When they arrived at the altar, everyone took their seats. Chase finally turned and looked at Carrie. The look on her face was priceless. It was one of complete and utter shock. She started running back down the aisle, only to trip on the horrendous thing she called a dress. Unfortunately, she didn't take a total spill. We moved to greet her in the lobby.

She pointed her bony finger at me. "You!" she yelled.

"Haven't we done this before, Carrie? It's not a wand."

She started screeching; what a horrid sound it was.

"Damn, girl, are you a fire detector? 'Cause you're really fucking loud and annoying," Jackson said.

Carrie moved to take a step towards me, but Ellie stepped in. "If karma doesn't hit you, I fucking will, you lying bitch." She was nose to nose with her. Carrie started to look unwell. I had a feeling the laxatives were about to make their presence known.

"Why?" Noah asked.

"I love you. It was supposed to be us all along."

281

"This isn't what you do to someone you love. If you really loved me, you would have done what Jules did. She left. It killed her to do it, but she wanted me to do what was right. She did it because she *loves* me. That is what love is really about. It's about sacrifice and putting the ones you love before yourself. You know nothing about love, Carrie. *Nothing.* I'm actually ashamed that I even entertained the thought of marrying you. After this is over, I never want to see your face again." He looked her square in the eyes. "I don't believe in hate. I think it weighs you down, but you're my exception. *I hate you.* I hate what you've done to me, and more than that, what you've done to the people I love. You disgust me," he said.

Just then, she grabbed her stomach and shit herself. It was disgustingly epic.

Noah grabbed my hand and walked away from her. He didn't even look back. Robert apologized again, saying he'd be in touch. I felt bad for him. He had a psycho bitch for a daughter and a spiteful, vindictive bitch for a sister-in-law.

The rest of us made plans to meet at Jackson's in a couple hours. Noah and I needed a little time alone first. Once we were back at his condo, exhaustion hit me full force. He picked me up as if I weighed nothing and carried me to the bedroom. I laughed when I noticed nothing had changed. All of my things were exactly how I had left them.

"She never came here," he said, reading my mind. "You belong here, Jules. You've belonged here all along. I didn't sleep with her, I promise."

"Nothing happened with Chase, either. Other than the kiss, but you already knew about that."

"I just want to hold you for a little while. Who am I kidding? I want to hold you like this forever." He pulled me snugly against him, so we were face to face.

We stayed like that for a long time until I drifted off. I was sleeping soundly until my stomach started rumbling. Noah helped me to my feet. We decided it was time to head to Jackson's where there was food. We headed down to the parking garage and I saw my car parked next to Noah's Jeep.

He shrugged. "I drove it back. With Chase in tow." I couldn't do anything but shake my head.

We climbed into the Jeep and headed to Jackson's apartment. When we arrived, everyone was cheerful. They were happy to see our reign of misery come to an end. I was still exhausted, but it was nice to see them. We laughed and joked around like nothing had

283

happened. At the end of the night, we made plans to catch up again tomorrow when I was better rested.

Finally, Noah and I headed *home.*

I jumped in the shower and changed into a pair of boyshorts and a tank top and then I climbed into bed. *Oh, how I've missed this bed.* Noah wrapped his arms around me and I was asleep instantly.

I woke up the next morning with Noah between my legs. He lifted his head and grinned. "I couldn't wait anymore. I feel like I've been in a desert since you left. I'm like a starving man at a buffet."

He resumed until I was gripping the bed sheets. We made slow, passionate love for most of the morning. We talked in between sessions. We were both on the same page. It was as if this had brought us even closer. It proved how strong our bond truly was. He asked if it was okay if we headed home next weekend to visit his parents, mostly his mom. She was extremely worried when he'd called to tell her to cancel her flight, and that the wedding was going to be called off. Of course, I agreed. I had always loved June. She had been like my adopted mother growing up.

The next day, we made arrangements to go to Atlanta at the end of the week. Robert called Noah to let him know that his brother was planning on filing for a divorce. They were also looking into the mysterious disappearance of Abigail's last husband, Clark. Noah put in his resignation from the firm. Robert was sad to see him go but offered his services if Noah ever needed them.

"I want to talk to you about something," Noah told me that night. "I want your honest opinion."

"That's all I ever give you, silly."

"I'm thinking of starting a new endeavor. I want to open my own firm. I know it's going to be hard, but I'm thinking about asking Joe to come with me."

"I think that's a wonderful idea. I'm proud of you."

Chapter Sixteen: 🔒 Unbreakable Heart

•◦•◦•◦•◦•◦•◦•◦•◦•◦•◦•◦•◦•◦•◦•◦•◦•

"Wake up, baby." Noah nudged me.

I opened my eyes and noticed that we were about to land. "Sorry. I'm up." I smiled brightly.

"Never apologize. I love watching you sleep."

Since we had flown first class, we were the first ones to exit the plane. Noah gathered our luggage, and we headed to pick up our rental car. We drove to where our childhood homes were. The week had been amazing. Joe had accepted Noah's offer, and they were already looking into possible office locations. He and Melissa had also announced that they were pregnant. I was so ecstatic for the both of them, especially given their fertility struggles. Jackson was taking Ellie upstate for the week, and she was excited to meet more of his family. It seemed like the Carrie episode was a thing of the past. I was so glad to have it behind us. Chase had even called to apologize.

"Hey, Jules," he'd said when I'd answered the phone.

287

"Chase."

"Listen, I know you don't want to talk to me, but I want to apologize."

"For what? Setting me up? Slashing my tires? Almost getting me kicked out of school? Lying to me? Leading me on? Pick one."

"It was never my intention to hurt you. You know I love you. I just wanted us to have another chance. I honestly thought that we had a shot." He had gone on to grovel for a few minutes. Even Noah thought I should forgive him.

"Listen, I forgive you, all right? I just don't want anything to do with you anymore."

"I understand. I'm sorry."

"Bye, Chase."

I looked out the window as Noah skillfully mastered his way through traffic. I couldn't believe how built up it had become since the last time I'd been here.

When we got to our neighborhood, I saw a little girl swinging on my swing in front of my childhood home. She looked at us and smiled. I walked over to her with Noah at my heels.

"Hi, I'm Jules. What's your name?" I said, crouching down to her height.

"Chloe," She was adorable. She had brown hair and freckles. She couldn't have been more than five.

"Chloe, did you know I used to live in that house?" I pointed to her house. "And I used to swing on this swing when I was your age."

"You did?" she asked with a huge grin.

"Yep."

"Do you want to swing on it?" She climbed off, and I couldn't resist. I sat on it and thought back to almost twenty years ago. The first time I had met Noah Sinclair, at this very spot. Chloe went to stand next to Noah.

"Want a push?" he asked.

This time, I said yes. He gave me a little push. We stayed and chatted with the Chloe for a couple more minutes and I thanked her for letting me use her swing. She said I could use it whenever I wanted.

Noah and I walked hand-in-hand to his house and knocked on the door. June answered with an enormous smile and pulled me into a bear hug. For being so small, she sure was strong. I hugged her back. Noah's dad, John, came into the foyer and stole me away from June.

"Baby girl. Look at you." He pulled away for a minute so he could get a good look at me. He crushed me into another hug. "We've missed you."

"I've missed you guys, too."

June ordered us into the kitchen and served us pie, just like she used to do when we were little. Noah recapped everything that had happened and June had a few choice words for Carrie. They were both over the moon, though, that we were back together.

I excused myself for a couple minutes to freshen up when the tough stuff was going to come out. I knew Noah was going to get into details about why I couldn't have children. I was in the powder room when June tapped on the door.

"Jules. Can I come in?" she asked.

"Sure." I opened the door. She had tears rolling down her cheeks. I was trying to hold mine at bay.

"I had no idea, honey. I'm so sorry you had to suffer through something like that. You were nothing more than a child yourself. I didn't know that you used to sleep here because you were scared to

290

be home. If I had known, I would have done something." I could tell she was beating herself up.

"There was nothing you could have done. It's okay now. It doesn't define me. If anything, it made me a better person," I said.

"Still, I wish I would have known. I really am happy for you both. He was miserable after you left, both times."

"Thank you. I love him more than I ever thought I could love anyone. I'm not going anywhere this time," I promised.

She hugged me and we went to join the men in the kitchen.

"Let me take you kids out to dinner," John said.

"Actually, we have other plans. We'll be gone for the night." I looked at him, shocked, but he played coy. That's when I noticed that he'd never brought our luggage in.

We said our goodbyes and headed back to the car. He produced something from his suit pocket. It was a blindfold. He gently put it on.

"You're in for a lot of surprises tonight."

Noah

It had felt nice to get everything out into the open with my parents. I thought my mom was going to have a heart attack when I told her that Jules had spent five years sleeping at our house because she was too scared to be at home. She was even more shocked to find out that we didn't have sex until the night before she'd left.

When I told her about Jules losing the baby, she was heartbroken. The worst was when I told them how she'd lost it. My mom was furious. She couldn't understand how someone could do something like that. My dad looked like he was going to kill something. He actually punched a hole in the wall. He even cried. My dad was a big guy, but he'd always had a soft spot for Jules.

I hugged them both and told them it was only going to be positive things from here on out.

With Jules blindfolded in the seat next to me, I pulled up to the Four Seasons in Atlanta. I had managed to get reservations for the same room we'd had the last time we stayed here, ten years ago. As soon as we were at the valet station, I told Jules she could take the blindfold off. She gasped when she saw where we were.

"I want to recreate what happened here the last time, but I want the ending to be different this time," I said.

Her eyes watered over, and I knew I was on the right track. I helped her out of the rental car and headed to the desk to check us in. Once we were settled in our room, I told her to shower and get changed. I had more arrangements to finish.

When she appeared in the bedroom after her shower, she looked breathtaking. She was in a knee length white dress that Ellie had helped her pick out for our trip. It showed off just the right amount of skin. I couldn't wait to take it off of her later…

I snapped myself back to the task at hand. "You look simply stunning." I took her hand and made her do a little twirl.

"So do you," she said.

I had changed into a charcoal gray suit, white shirt, and black tie. It was almost the exact outfit I'd worn the last time. I looped her arm through mine as we headed down to Park 75 for dinner. We ordered the same dinners we had ten years ago. When the peanut butter lava cake came out, I felt my palms start to get sweaty.

I stood up and dropped to one knee. All eyes were on me. "Julia Kline, you've spent your whole life running. All you've done is run farther away from the love that's been waiting for you all

293

along. The first time you smiled at me with your two missing teeth, you had my undivided love and attention. When you laugh, I want to laugh with you. When you cry, I want to be the one to hold you. The first time you said you loved me, you hijacked my heart forever. They say that love is the condition in which the happiness of another person is essential to your own. Your happiness is what I will spend the rest of my life striving to give you. I love you so much. Will you do the honor of marrying me?" I asked.

I produced the ring from my pocket as she placed her hand in mine. I may have gone a little overboard, but as far as she was concerned, my wallet seemed to know no bounds. I'd had it custom-made by a friend of Randall's. The band was platinum, and the center held a five-carat cushion cut diamond surrounded by more bead-set diamonds. I loved it and it screamed Jules. She probably would have preferred something from a vending machine, or, at least, something in the single figures, but I wanted to do this for her. I will string Jackson up by his balls if he ever tells her how much I spent on it.

"Yes!" The room erupted in applause and the server brought over a bottle of pink champagne and poured two glasses.

"To the first day of the rest of our lives," I toasted her. We clinked glasses and enjoyed our dessert before returning to our room.

I'd had the room filled with pink peonies and tea-lights while we were at dinner.

She gasped when she walked into the room. 'Lucky' by Jason Mraz was playing softly in the background. I stood behind her and reminded her how lucky I was to have her, my best friend and my future wife. I slid off her white dress and made love to my fiancé. It was perfect.

When we woke up the next morning, there was no worrying about running to the airport. There were no goodbyes. Just I love you. "What would you say if I wanted to get married in a week?" I asked her.

"A week? Like Vegas?" She cocked an eyebrow.

"Not exactly. See, Ellie and Jackson are kind of upstate setting everything up… if it's not what you want, though, we can wait," I said.

"I've waited long enough." She leaned in until her lips met mine.

295

Chapter Seventeen: Wedding Bells

Jules ♥

"I swear you guys have had the shortest engagement out of anyone I've known, except maybe Brittany Spears," Ellie joked, pinning my veil. "This was a lot to pull off in a week, but everything looks amazing! I'm so happy for you both."

I hugged her gratefully. She was serving as my maid of honor and Melissa was serving as my bridesmaid. Jackson was Noah's best man and Joe was his groomsman. It had worked out perfectly. Noah told me that, when we were planning the engagement, he hadn't wanted to wait to get married. He also knew that I wouldn't want a cheesy Vegas wedding, so when Randall offered up his house upstate, he couldn't say no. Ellie and Jackson had been here all week making sure everything was in order and waiting for our out of town guests. We had wanted something small with just our family and our closest friends.

"Can I have a minute with the beautiful lady?" my dad asked.

"Sure, Alex. I'm finished here anyway." Ellie ducked out of the room, closing the door behind her.

"I need to apologize to you," he said. "I had no idea what I was leaving you with. I wasn't a great father to you. I know I can't change the past, but I'd really like to change the future."

"I'd like that," I said and I hugged him.

In Atlanta, I had called to check in with Harry and told him about the engagement. An hour later, my dad had called, and we'd finally cleared the air. I felt a lot lighter these days. He was thrilled about the engagement. He said he'd always liked Noah. I had even asked him to walk me down the aisle. He was a little shocked when I told him that the wedding was taking place in a week, but he said he wouldn't miss it. They had arrived two days ago. I was happy when Noah took an instant liking to Harry.

My father and I linked arms and headed down the hallway to the stairwell. I looked to where the altar had been set up. The music started playing and we slowly marched to where Noah stood, waiting. He looked dashing in his black tux. I loved my simple lace dress. It looked very elegant and hugged my curves; it also hadn't needed any alterations.

The priest asked who gave me away and my dad said he did with tears in his eyes. He lifted my veil and kissed my cheek before placing my hand in Noah's. I took my last step forward as Julia Kline.

"We are gathered here today to witness the marriage of Noah James Sinclair and Julia Victoria Kline." The priest cleared his throat. "Sometimes people come into your lives and you just know that they're the ones you are meant to be with. That's the case with Noah and Jules. Their story started almost twenty years ago. Marriage is more than joining the bonds of two people. It's the uniting of two souls already attuned to each other. Please recite your vows to one another."

"Jules," Noah said, "from the moment I first saw you, I knew you were the one I wanted to share my life with. Your beauty, heart, and mind inspire me to be the best person I can be. I promise to love you for eternity. Respecting you, honoring you, and sharing my life with you. I promise to always treat you with kindness, unselfishness, and trust. I will work by your side to create a wonderful life together. I take you, Jules, to be my lawful wife, to have and to hold, from this day forward, for better or worse, in sickness and in health, as long as we both shall live."

299

"Noah, in your eyes I have found my home. In your heart, I have found my love. In your soul, I have found my mate. With you, I am whole, full, and alive. You make me laugh. You let me cry. I am yours, and you are mine; of this, we are certain. I promise to respect and support you, to be patient and loving towards you, to work by your side to achieve the things we value and dream of, and to savor our time together. I pledge to you all of these things, from the bottom of my heart, for the rest of our lives. I take you, Noah, to be my lawful husband, to have and to hold, from this day forward, for better or worse, in sickness and in health, as long as we both shall live."

The minister started his ring speech. "Having this kind of love in your hearts, you have chosen to share a ring as a sign and seal of the vows you made today. Though small in size, a ring has large significance. It's made of precious metal, and it reminds us that love is not cheap nor common. Made in a circle, the design tells us that love must never come to an end. We must keep it continuous. As you wear your rings, whether together or apart for a moment, may they be constant reminders of the promises you made today. Please recite your ring vow."

"As this ring has no end, neither does my love for you," Noah and I said at the same time, sliding our rings into place.

"May you always need one another," the priest continued, "not so much to fill the emptiness but to help each other know your fullness. May you want one another, but not out of lack. May you embrace one another, but not encircle one another. May you succeed in all-important ways with one another and not fail in little graces. Look for things to praise. Say I love you, and say it often." He looked to our small crowd. "It is my pleasure to introduce Mr. and Mrs. Noah Sinclair. You may kiss your bride."

Noah raised his hand to my cheek and lowered his lips to mine. Our lips met tenderly at first but the kiss ended impassioned. It was magical. When we rounded the corner, I was shocked to see the dining room had been transformed into a banquet room with several tables. The table cloths were dove gray with pale pink napkins and accents. The centerpieces were pink peonies. It was intimate, and it was just how I'd envisioned it.

We chatted with some of our guests before taking our seats. Jackson tapped his glass and prepared for his best man toast. He cleared his throat.

"Noah, you have been my best friend for the past nine years. We have been through a lot together, not all of it has been happy or great. When I first met you, all you talked about was this girl named Jules. I wondered what could possibly make her so special. Until I met her. She's sharp and says things how they are, not to mention

301

the fact that, on a scale of one to ten, she's a twelve. Why she wants a doofus like you is beyond me, but she does. As your best friend, I couldn't be happier. A wise man once told me that the best man's speech should be as long as the groom makes love. Thank you, ladies and gentleman." He started to sit down. "Oh, and never go to bed angry."

Ellie stood next. "For those of you who don't know me, my name is Ellie. Jules and I have been best friends, more like sisters really, for the past ten years. Our friendship has spanned the awkward and challenging high school years, the independent and demanding college years, and the difficult yet rewarding grad school years. I look forward to the years beyond all of that, when we are entering the next phase of our lives. In the time that we've known each other, Jules and I have usually lived about twenty feet apart, but regardless of distance, neither of us has ever taken our friendship for granted. We're sisters at heart and we have been there for each other through some pretty difficult times. We've given each other support through life's struggles. We've been there for each other through the good times, too. Throughout the past ten years, we've spent our time learning what we wanted to do with our lives. Today, we are celebrating one of the best days of Jules' life, her marriage to the man whom she's loved all her life. That's you, Noah. You're a very lucky man, but you already knew that. I'm thrilled for you both, and if you hurt her, I will hunt you to the ends of the Earth, Mr. Sinclair." She beamed and took a seat in Jackson's lap.

There were only about thirty people at the reception. We enjoyed our dinners and had opted for cupcakes instead of a tradition cake. The day was perfect.

"What do you say we bail and head out on our honeymoon, Mrs. Sinclair?" Noah asked.

"I like the way you think, Mr. Sinclair." I kissed him as we headed to the waiting car.

Epilgoue

Three and a half years later...

I woke up feeling like I'd peed myself. Then I realized it was time! "Noah," I whispered. "Wake up. It's time."

He shot up like a bolt of lightning and started tripping over his feet. It was adorable to see him all worked up.

"Relax, we have a while yet. I need to call Ellie. Can you call Melissa?" I asked calmly. I picked up my phone.

"Hewo," Ellie mumbled, still sleeping. I could picture her face in the pillow, making me laugh.

"It's time," I said. It was like a jolt of caffeine for her.

"Oh my gosh, really? We're on our way." I heard her slap Jackson awake. She didn't have far to go since Noah and Jackson had bought adjoining pieces of property on the outskirts of Amityville. They had built houses next to each other.

Jackson and Ellie had finally tied the knot last year, and she was three months pregnant with their first. After we'd returned from our honeymoon, Melissa had wanted to try a new procedure to reduce the scarring. It took us a year and a half to get pregnant with our son, Jackson James Sinclair, who was nestled in his bed now. When we found out we were pregnant again, we were both shocked.

I remembered when I had told Noah. He had just come in from the office and walked into our family room, where little Jax was pulling himself up. He had just started doing it about an hour before. There was no stopping him now.

"Did you see that?" Noah cooed as Jax pulled himself up on the coffee table and smiled a gummy grin. Noah was beaming like the proud dad he was. "He's getting so big already." He walked up to him and gave Jax a hug. I was wondering how long it was going to take him until he read his onesie. It took all of a minute in a half.

"I'm going to be a big brother," Noah read and looked at me with wide eyes. I nodded and started getting emotional. He came to pull me into a kiss. "Really?"

"Really."

The labor pains quickly snapped me out of my reverie. Ellie was already here and she walked into the bedroom. Apparently, Uncle Jackson was asleep on the couch. She was going to the hospital with us while Jackson stayed here to look after their godson.

Noah loaded the overnight bags into the car and helped me in. We sped to the hospital much faster than necessary. He checked us in and they came to wheel me up to labor and delivery. I wanted to walk; sitting was just too uncomfortable.

Melissa met us a few minutes later and checked me. "Wow, you're already eight centimeters. We're having a baby."

"Already?" Noah asked.

"Yes. I need to prep." She called the nurses and went to scrub at the sink.

Twenty-minutes later, and after only a handful of pushes, much different than my labor with Jax, our daughter, Gracie Mae Sinclair, was born. Noah cut the cord with tears in his eyes. Melissa cleaned her off and handed her to me. She was beautiful. She had little cherub cheeks, blue eyes like her daddy and blonde hair like me.

With her on my chest, I was in awe and completely in love all over again. It's amazing what love can do. Even more miraculous how one little person could work his or her way into your heart and fill a void you never knew existed in the first place.

Over the years, I never thought of my own mother anymore. Instead, I focused all my love and energy on being the best mother I could be. It did eventually come out from Robert that Clark's disappearance wasn't exactly a mystery; Abigail had been trying to swindle him out of his money, so he just took off. They tracked him down in Cabo happily sipping margaritas. I was glad he escaped her clutches too.

Two days later, we finally got to return home with our new bundle of joy. Pulling up out front, I couldn't help the smile that spread across my face. Our house had taken over a year and a half to build and I absolutely loved it. It wasn't anything extravagant, but it was exactly what we needed. We had four bedrooms. Turns out adding the extra bedroom at the last minute had been a good thing after all, especially since we managed to fill three rather quickly. The only thing that I'd cared about was having a good size kitchen and family room. We had a nice backyard that the boys had completely fenced in to include Jackson and Ellie's as well, creating one giant space.

Noah gave his condo to Harry, who was attending NYU. I loved having him close, and he was a great uncle to Jax.

Opening the door with the baby carrier in hand, we were greeted by a toothy grin from Jax. He was sitting with his Uncle Harry and Uncle Jackson. He immediately walked over to the carrier to take a peek. "Baby," he said, pointing.

"Yes. Baby Gracie," I said softly.

"Gracie," he repeated.

I was so proud. He was so smart and kind. He looked exactly like a mini version of Noah. Hugging him tightly, I told him how much I loved him. I hugged Harry and smacked Jackson, who made a smartass remark about my boobs. Ellie cooed over her new goddaughter.

Later, everyone gathered around the dining room table for dinner and then I tucked Jax in for the night and read him a story. "This is my wish for you. Comfort on difficult days, smiles when sadness intrudes, rainbows to chase the clouds away, laughter to kiss your lips, sunsets to warm your heart, hugs when spirits sag, beauty for your eyes to see, friendships to brighten your being, faith so that you can believe, confidence for you when you doubt, courage to know yourself, patience to accept the truth, and love to complete your life. I love you, baby boy," I told him as he drifted off to sleep.

I kissed his sleeping face and turned to see Noah holding Gracie in the doorway.

"I love you, Mrs. Sinclair," he whispered.

"I love you, Mr. Sinclair."

What makes life worth living is knowing that, one day, you'll wake up and find the person who makes you happier than anything in the whole world. So don't ever lose hope and give up. Everything turns out okay, and the good guy always wins. I'm a firm believer in second chances. If we're going to go through life not giving anyone a second chance, what kind of life are we going to have?

310

First and as always, *thank you* so much for reading! Writing is a journey. I've always equated it to bleeding on paper. This was one of the first books that I ever wrote and I still have the same feeling of awe and fear with every push of the publish button. Second, there's way too many people to thank and show love to, if you're reading this, you're one of them! I'd like to thank my best friends for sticking by me and my quirky ways every day, not just while I'm writing. And for understanding my need to live in a blanketfort bubble and sometimes not returning texts until days later. This is why Skittles (aka Danielle Jamie) and I click! Plus, you're about to find out what we've been waiting months to shout to the world...

To find out what I'm up to next, you can find me on Facebook at:

www.facebook.com/sophiemonroewrites

www.sophiemonroewrites.com

Here's a first look at **Candy Hearts**, a new serial that I (we) cannot wait to get to you guys!

Danielle Jamie's Scandalous book has opened the gates to the Candy Heart app. After spending a much-needed girls weekend at a cabin in Upstate NY, we decided it would make a fantastic serial. With that, myself and my best friend and Bestselling Author, Danielle Jamie are bringing you another scandalous serial about four candy heart girls who just so happen to be best friends and sorority sisters at Columbia University!

Over the next twelve months, you'll dive into the world of Raelyn, Valerie, Megan and Emmy. Four friends and four of New York City's highest paid escorts and Candy Heart's most sought after girls. They're beautiful, young and carefree. Living double lives in order to keep up with the rich and famous lifestyle of the city that never sleeps.

The last thing any of them is looking for is love—but that's the crazy thing about love—it seems to find you when you least expect it.

Book 1 introduces you to all four girls and gives you the start to Valerie's story! We are so excited to introduce these four friends to the reading world.

Valerie Martin appears to be much like any other college student. She's studying law, belongs to a sorority and looks just like every other girl-next-door. With her busy life and aspiring dreams the last thing she's looking for is love, but under the pretty surface is a secret that could destroy everything that she's worked for.

Wesley 'Wes' Brooks is one of Manhattan's most eligible, wealthiest bachelors. Rich, handsome and successful, he's not sure real

312

"love" is in the cards for him. After spending years in the tabloids and living the dream, he's left feeling lonely and unfulfilled. For months, his friends kept telling him to try out this new app they're all on called Candy Hearts. Against his better judgment, one-drunken night he does. Could a twist of fate send unexpected love skyrocketing, or will this romance end in a fiery crash?

Fated Hearts Playlist:

Halestorm- What Sober Couldn't Say
Black Stone Cherry- Runaway
Stone Sour- Wicked Game
Luke Bryan- Just Over
Brad Paisley- Perfect Storm
The Gaslight Anthem- Get Hurt
Cam- Burning House
Mayday Parade- Hold onto Me
Thomas Rhett- Die A Happy Man
Meghan Trainor- Like I'm Gonna Lose You

For More of what I'm
listening to and full
playlists, follow me on
Spotify @ sophiemonroe07